SEVERED ROOTS

A Paper Spider Production
Vaughan, Ontario, Canada

SEVERED ROOTS

a dystopian novel

NEGO HUZCOTOQ

Copyright © 2023 Nego Huzcotoq

All rights reserved.

No part of this book may be reproduced or used in any manner without the written permission of the publisher except for the use of quotations in a book review.

This is a work of fiction. Names, characters, places, and incidents either are the product of the author's imagination or are used fictitiously. Any resemblance to actual persons, living or dead, events, or locales is entirely coincidental.

Print ISBN: 978-1-7386781-0-5

E-book ISBN: 978-1-7386781-1-2

The family. We were a strange little band of characters trudging through life sharing diseases and toothpaste, coveting one another's desserts, hiding shampoo, borrowing money, locking each other out of our rooms, inflicting pain and kissing to heal it in the same instant, loving, laughing, defending, and trying to figure out the common thread that bound us all together.

—Erma Bombeck

PROLOGUE

It was not a movement the government had created. It was not a movement led by a dictator or despot. It was not even a movement that had been started solely by women. It was, rather, a movement of an entire species frustrated with the intractable problem of men—what to do with them, how to tame them, how to prevent them from destroying the world. It was, in essence, a movement of the whole against half of itself. It was a grassroots movement born and nurtured in freedom and democracy by a people that had long lost its way—a movement born of necessity, perhaps, but whose goals required a radical break from the past, including the consensual, gradual, snuffing out of half of humankind.

—Domenico Rocca, *The Making of the New World Order*
(Preface to the expanded edition).

CHAPTER ONE

Nick Wong strutted through his downtown Ottawa neighbourhood, grinning as he basked in the success of his performance last night: The jaw drops when he passed a saltshaker through the table. The screams-turned-belly laughter when he sneezed and his head appeared to fall off his neck. Most of all, Nick relished the memory of the long-faced, scrunched up woman in the wheelchair, the dying embers in her eyes lighting up as he transported her to a world where limitations were illusions and troubles could be forgotten.

Before long, the grin on Nick's face vanished.

It happened when several women in navy blue pants and crisp gold shirts strode past him, their gazes flitting. Their refusal to make eye contact made him feel like a discarded pop can—empty and crushed.

Reality had set in. It always did.

He sighed and turned into Amazon Mall.

The line in front of Simple Wear snaked down the main aisle of the shopping centre. A procession of mankeys like himself, in old sweatshirts and shapeless pants, shuffled into the store. Joining the queue, Nick focused on the monitor hanging from the ceiling.

"Despite a heavy police presence," the anchorwoman's voice blared, "the Hardinians on Parliament Hill broke through the crowd-control barriers, allowing other insurgents to pour through..."

More violence.

He wished he were still in bed. But today was Saturday, and Age of Oppression Memorial Day was in three days. All males sixteen and over had to wear pink slippers or risk a hefty fine. His old pair had ripped.

Nick studied the line, only marginally shorter now. His feet sweltered in his sneakers, and his lower back ached. The smell of freshly baked dough, garlic and cheese wafting from the food court made his stomach grumble.

Ape-brain. Should have eaten more before leaving my apartment.

He looked again at the monitor, hoping to get his mind off the hunger. "...latest statistics from the World Federation indicate the male population has declined 14.8 percent in the last twelve months, slightly slower than planned..."

Nick yawned. He arched his back and was stretching and twisting to loosen it after standing for so long when something caught his eye: Beatrice, sitting on a bench about thirty feet away, bulky shopping bags on either side.

Strange—her usually neatly groomed, shoulder-length hair hung disheveled.

They'd met last summer at her boss's backyard birthday party. Nick had been hired to do magic tricks.

"You were awesome," Beatrice had said after his performance, warmth radiating from her round, dimpled face. Her own birthday was approaching, she'd added, and Nick's show had helped lift her spirits.

They had begun a long conversation, the subject of which he no longer recalled. He only remembered laughing and nodding and watching Beatrice listen to his every word.

Since that first encounter, he'd enjoyed all their conversations and secretly considered her his best friend. She was different from every other woman: she respected his ideas. But today, Nick didn't want to lose his position in the queue and hoped she wouldn't notice him.

As he contemplated how he could make himself invisible, Beatrice looked up and their eyes met. She waved.

Dang.

Nick waved back, frowning while pointing to the long line of people that had formed behind him. She tilted her head, as though confused.

Hmm...can't expect her to saunter over with those heavy bags. After shifting his weight from one foot to the other a few times, he sighed and walked toward her.

He stopped midstride. Her face was streaked with tears.

"W-what happened?" Nick glanced around, assuring himself no one else was within earshot. It would be awkward for a mankey to be seen trying to console a woman.

"Earlier...in the washroom...I was grabbed from behind."

"What?"

"It was awful. I was so scared I couldn't scream. She pulled my hair and dug her fingernails into my scalp. Felt like she was pushing razor blades under my skin." Beatrice's chin trembled. "She called me a 'pervert' and a 'mankey lover.'"

Nick flinched.

"I turned and there were two more of them. They told me they recognized me from last night's Women's Meeting, saying my behaviour was deplorable and they'd file a complaint with the Ministry."

"A complaint?" Nick swallowed and stepped closer. "What'd you do?

"I spoke my mind."

"And?"

"And what?"

Severed Roots

"There's freedom of speech—"

Beatrice snorted. "Not for promoting sanity." She grabbed a grocery bag and was about to move it off the bench.

"Oh, I'm fine." Nick held up his hand. While he appreciated her intention, it wasn't proper for a mankey to sit too close to a woman.

He remained standing, attentive to Beatrice's every word, facial expression and gesture as she related the previous evening's disturbing events.

How Beatrice hated these local Women's Meetings. As soon as she arrived at the old school gymnasium, she glanced at her watch: 8:44 p.m. *Fourteen minutes late, perfect.* She had timed her arrival well. Fifteen minutes late would have resulted in a reprimand.

Although these monthly gatherings always started a half hour late, people were expected to arrive on time. Unfortunately, the only access was from the front, so everyone who walked in faced those already seated. Beatrice scanned the gymnasium, which was almost filled to capacity. Taking a deep breath, she marched down the aisle toward an empty chair near the back, below a corroded, upturned basketball hoop. She took her seat, hoping no one would try to strike up a conversation or offer her a joint while waiting for the meeting to start. The scent of weed was stronger than usual that evening.

Despite the hard plastic chair, Beatrice refrained from fidgeting. She looked alternately at the floor, the dusty bare walls, the grinding ceiling fan, and the two front loudspeakers—anything to avoid seeing the imposing glass-framed portrait of the Advisor, the head of the World Federation.

Beatrice shuddered every time she saw the Advisor's image: the wispy strands of cotton-white hair; the thousand wrinkles that went every which way and even crisscrossed each other; the deep, dark eye sockets. The Advisor looked as if she were resurrected from a bygone era, yet the fierce ambition in her eyes and smile suggested a creature who belonged to the present and, even more, to the future.

The air remained stale despite the ceiling fan. No one else seemed bothered. People looked ahead placidly, some occasionally taking a puff or leaning to one side and exchanging a few words with their neighbours.

Beatrice slid a sandaled foot back and forth along the smooth vinyl flooring, and soon her breathing slowed. Decades ago, a teenager probably dribbled a basketball on the same spot where Beatrice placed her foot. And some young child surely landed a sneaker there while jumping or sprinting in a relay race.

Alas, that was before her time. Before they sent the children to live in Children's Centres.

It's not right. This gymnasium was built for kids to play in, not for these asinine Women's Meetings.

Drumbeats rolled through the room. Two women wearing navy blue suits and gold headbands strode in. One, with cropped hair, turned and pointed a finger at the wall behind her. A familiar image appeared: a solid orange circle partially eclipsing a solid black circle and the words *Our Future Is Near.*

The drumming ceased.

Everyone rose. The two women chanted, "Our future is near." The audience, including Beatrice, joined in. This went on for thirty agonizing seconds.

The crop-haired woman signaled everyone to sit.

"Friends," she cried, "our future is near! We will recite the Five Principles. I would like a volunteer." Many hands shot up. She flashed a cold smile. "How about the person in the back with the blond hair who arrived late?" She locked eyes with Beatrice. "Would you please stand?"

Beatrice's heart raced. Heads turned, and she felt the crushing gaze of a hundred sets of eyes. She rose from her chair.

"Your name, please."

"B-Beatrice Tender."

"Well, B-Beatrice Tender." A sprinkling of laughter rose from the audience. "You have the honour of reciting the defining principles of our Movement."

Beatrice clenched her jaw. To decline would mean a lengthy interrogation. She kept her voice low. "The first principle of the Movement is, The nature of mankeys is to control and abuse women." She swallowed. "The second principle of the Movement is, Our higher status is our due for centuries of selflessness and sacrifice. The third—"

"Beatrice, please recite each principle without prefacing it."

Beatrice paused. She had hoped she could get away with saying them in an impersonal manner. She tightened her fists until her nails bit into her palms.

"We shall never give power back to mankeys." Her voice quivered. "Family threatens social harmony and productivity. We shall not be intimate with mankeys but only with other women."

Beatrice sat, blood pounding in her ears.

The second chant leader stepped up to the lectern. She removed the joint dangling from her mouth and cleared her throat.

"Ladies, we are at a time in history where we have advanced ahead of mankeys. They have become evolutionary failures." She raised a fist, and the crowd cheered. "But we have much work still to do if we want world peace. We must continue to accumulate power." She looked over the audience with hungry eyes. "We must win over countries stuck in the past, where Hardinians have a foothold..."

Ten minutes later, she concluded. "Fellow fighters, the insurgency is gaining momentum, even here in Canada. We must remain vigilant. The enemy is everywhere. They could be your friends, your next-door neighbours...even someone in this room." Her voice shook with fierce determination. "We must continue our struggle for a peaceful world, a world where our bright orange sun eclipses the blackness of mankeys' ignorance and brutality. I now turn the floor over to Karla Rook, Senior Project Officer at the Ministry of Tomorrow."

A broad-shouldered woman sporting jet-black hair and a fleshy nose with an upturned tip advanced to the lectern. She adjusted her navy blue suit and straightened her blood-red tie.

Beatrice slid her sweaty palms back and forth along the sides of her seat and braced herself for another verbal onslaught.

"Our future is near," Karla bellowed.

"Our future is near," the auditorium reverberated.

"Our future is near!" she shouted louder, a clenched fist in front of her face.

"Our future is near," the audience screamed.

Beatrice had seen Karla at previous meetings. She was always pumped up.

"As you know, this Tuesday is Age of Oppression Memorial Day, and we expect no less than full participation. You all have your assigned tasks. I shouldn't have to remind you that if you see a mankey on the street not wearing pink slippers, you must notify the police. Issuing a warning is not enough anymore."

Beatrice gritted her teeth.

Someone's hand went up in the audience. Karla pivoted. "Yes…Charlene?"

A small, white-haired woman rose. "It's Charlotte. I was just thinking. It doesn't seem right that in a free country some people are forced to wear a certain type of footwear. It didn't use to be that way."

Karla scanned the audience, undoubtedly seeing many annoyed faces, before returning her steady eyes to the elderly woman.

"Thank you, Charlotte, for sharing your perspective. But it's the law. We might as well also ask why these monthly meetings are obligatory. Or why, in a court of law, everyone must stand when the judge enters. Or why we allow peaceful demonstrations against the government but not ones that incite violence. Sometimes freedoms need to be curtailed for the greater good."

"Ahh. Makes sense." The old woman sat.

Severed Roots

Karla stared at her for several seconds before turning her attention to the rest of the audience. "As I was saying, you all have your assigned tasks for this Tuesday. As for next year's Memorial Day, we will build on lessons learned. But the Ministry of Tomorrow has added a new theme: mankeys' brutality against children. We'll be looking to you for ideas."

Children? Fury ignited in Beatrice's gut. *Society has gone mad.* She sprang up. "I—"

Heads turned. She froze. Her impulsiveness had shot out of her legs and mouth. Her knees weakened.

"Yes, Beatrice?" Karla said.

It was too late to back down. Everyone stared, waiting. She needed to say something. She rocked from side to side. "I would like to be the first to share my ideas."

"Yes, Beatrice?"

Beatrice felt light-headed. She wanted to sit but couldn't. It was as if everyone's eyes were propping her up, preventing her from resuming her seat.

"This...I think this...crusade against men—mankeys—is going too far." Beatrice imagined the audience filled with vultures and snakes, waiting to pounce on her as soon as she stumbled. "It may not be...necessary. Mankeys have no real contact with children."

Murmurs swept across the room. Karla strutted down the aisle, over the faded black and red lines on the gymnasium floor, cementing an icy stare on Beatrice. Her shoulders were pressed back, her stride long and commanding.

When she reached Beatrice's row, she stopped and faced her. "And do you not know, Beatrice, that the reason we forbid nonwomen to be alone with children is precisely because of their proclivity to control and abuse them?"

Beatrice trembled, yet she was determined to stand her ground. "I'm sure not all men are like that. If I ever have a child—uh, I mean, if that were legal—I would want a man to help me raise it. A man who cared about children and wouldn't harm them."

Many in the room gaped, others winced.

"I mean"—she swallowed hard—"there's *got* to be a few mankeys like that in the world."

Dead silence prickled her nerves. The only sound was the rhythmic grinding of the overhead fan. Beatrice sat and waited, her stomach a jumble of knots.

The universe had paused, needing to figure out its next move.

After a long moment, a tall, husky woman in a middle row got up and made her way ostentatiously to the lectern. Turning to the audience, she looked straight at Beatrice. She positioned her mouth very close to the microphone, almost tasting it. "You are a *wife*," she hissed and then returned to her seat.

Nick stared, mouth agape, as Beatrice finished her story.

"I was shocked. I've never been called a wife before." Tears welled in Beatrice's eyes. "She said it to a room full of people! I felt worse than dirt."

Nick's pulse thrummed in his temples. At least it had been a member of the audience, and not Karla, who'd called Beatrice a wife. No—Karla would never do such a thing. Nick had known Karla since childhood; she was always respectful to everyone. A passionate defender of freedom of speech, she was one of the few women Nick dared engage with on contentious topics.

"Why did you speak out in the first place?"

"I couldn't contain myself."

Nick's throat constricted. "Then what happened?"

"Nothing. I could hardly breathe. I don't remember anything more except, vaguely, being on my feet during the final chanting. I stared at the back of the chair in front of me until I felt a squeeze on my arm and someone said it was time to go home."

Nick remained standing in front of Beatrice as if his sneakers were glued to the tiles. *Don't cry*, he wanted to tell her. He searched his pockets for a tissue but couldn't find any. He felt useless.

"It was that old lady, Charlotte," Beatrice said flatly. "She told me she was once an oddball and that I, too, will see the light."

Beatrice stared at the floor, sniffling. "Why can't a woman have a baby of her own?" She wiped her cheeks with her hands. "Why must it be a crime? Weren't women given wombs?"

Nick straightened. He glanced around to make sure no one was paying attention to them. His eyes settled on Beatrice's quivering lower lip. Although Nick knew there were women who wanted to be mothers, they were rare. Yes, he'd heard some women say it, but it was always said in jest. Beatrice was serious.

His chest tightened and his stomach churned. Nick had been raised to believe a person should put society's needs first.

Is Beatrice selfish? In the months that he'd known her, her kindness had impressed him. Like the time she'd accompanied him home after one of his performances, when a headache skewed his vision and nauseated him. *Can it be that she is ignorant? Doesn't she understand the social harm of motherhood?*

Nick's stomach felt hollow. It grumbled and made him light-headed. He took a step back. "I-I need to go home and eat. It's pretty late."

Beatrice scrutinized his face with her puffy eyes. "Nick, I'll be thirty in August. Do you know how I'm going to celebrate my birthday?" Her expression dimmed.

Nick shrugged. Two years ago he'd announced to his buddies at the Mankey Bar that it was his thirtieth birthday. They had treated him to a Coke and a donut.

"I'm going to set myself on fire—in front of the Ministry building. You're invited to attend and bring all your friends. I no longer want to live in a world like this."

Nick stared at her, his neck muscles tensing. *Why is she telling me this? What am I supposed to do?* He wanted to yell at her, beg her to reconsider, but his mouth wouldn't cooperate. His thoughts froze and his body overheated. He craved fresh air.

He pretended he hadn't heard clearly.

"Anyway, it was nice seeing you," he stammered, taking a shaky step backward.

He continued to back up a few feet, avoiding eye contact, then turned and shambled toward the end of the snake line, a deserter trying to hide in a searchlight. Once out of Beatrice's line of sight, he stood still for a long time, every inch of his skin tingling. Then, he punched his fists against his thighs and headed straight for the exit.

CHAPTER TWO

As Nick walked toward the street, his legs felt numb, but he pressed on.

He'd abandoned Beatrice, his closest friend, in her time of need. But what could he have done? She was a woman. She could figure things out better without him. It was enough he'd left the queue for her.

Friendship was arbitrary and transient, like the news headlines. How many of his friends still kept in touch?

"A relationship is only as strong as the one who wants it the least," Beatrice had once said.

Still, he could have stayed longer, accompanied her home, maybe carried her grocery bags. He could have stayed a few more minutes to show—and to prove to himself—he cared.

Am I able to truly care for another person?

A heavy bitterness filled his chest. He thought about running back to Beatrice but didn't want to appear a fool. No, he'd wait for another opportunity to apologize. And he'd return for the pink slippers tomorrow.

Severed Roots

As Nick waited at the intersection for the pedestrian symbol to light up, his eyes were drawn to the same old billboard:

ARE YOU TIRED OF WALLOWING IN SELF-PITY BECAUSE YOU'RE A MANKEY?

- *BOLSTER YOUR SELF-ESTEEM!*
- *IMPROVE YOUR CAREER PROSPECTS!*
- *INCREASE YOUR SENSITIVITY AND COMPASSION!*

"Sensitivity and compassion"—exactly what I need. He squinted while reading the smaller lettering underneath.

Over 78,000 satisfied customers have benefited from our attractive package, which includes lifelong hormone replacement therapy, no-pain surgery, and two weeks of disability insurance. Generous government subsidies available. Visit womenRthefuture.com

Nick mentally noted the address and continued home. *Maybe it's time I finally took charge of my life.*

Nego Huzcotoq

The following morning, Nick lay in bed, staring at a new crack in the ceiling. The wall monitor beeped and lit up.

The bright, twelve-inch screen showed Karla. Eyebrows neatly trimmed, black hair pulled back in a bun.

Nick tensed. She rarely phoned him during the day. He sat up, his mattress squeaking, and turned on his camera.

"Hello, Nick. We need to talk."

"Uh, hi. What is it?" Even after all these years, Nick wasn't completely at ease around Karla. For some reason, their relationship never felt natural.

"Has your friend Beatrice spoken to you recently about wanting to be a mother?"

Nick's heart raced. He didn't want to get Beatrice in trouble, but it was wrong to lie, especially to a woman. If only he'd never told Karla about his friend!

"Why, uh, do you ask?" Nick's thick legs stretched out in front of him as he fumbled along the side of the mattress for his stash of Hershey's. Hidden from the camera's eye, his pudgy fingers closed around the sweets.

Severed Roots

"She said something at the last Women's Meeting that caused a bit of a stir. We're concerned about her mental health."

"I—I'm not... We're not that close. I mean, I don't even know what day her birthday is." Nick felt stupid for saying that; he also felt guilty. Beatrice was his best friend, and he knew only that her birthday was sometime in August.

"Okay. Keep your distance. She may turn to crime one day."

"Wh-what do you mean?"

"Some women with her condition become so desperate they apply for a job in human manufacturing, only to abscond with the child and raise it themselves."

Nick tried to imagine Beatrice as a criminal but drew a blank. "Don't they screen the surrogates before hiring them?"

"No system is perfect. Be cautious is all I'm saying." Karla paused. "Anyway, how's the high-powered career? Made any elephants disappear lately?"

She mocks me even though she's never attended any of my magic shows. A tingle of defiance crept up Nick's spine. "Sometimes I wish I could make *my past* disappear."

Karla fixed her hypnotic grey eyes on him. She must have known what he was alluding to—his years at the Children's Centre, the subject of many heated discussions between them.

"Be thankful you can't."

"Thankful?"

"Yes, thankful. Grateful. Appreciative." Her voice climbed higher with each adjective. "Parenting has ruined every generation since the dawn of humanity. Mothers knew better than fathers, of course, but the fathers held the power and made all the decisions."

"Are you saying"—Nick tried to shake off the remnant of his early morning drowsiness—"that not a single father was capable of raising children?" Ever since he could remember, Nick had been in awe of Karla's encyclopedic knowledge and had learned to ask questions rather than state his opinions.

"For goodness' sake, Nick. Books and seminars have existed forever on how to parent with love, respect, and good values, but the vast majority of mank—males didn't want to or were unable to change their habits." Karla raised a smug eyebrow at him.

"Well, enough is enough," Karla continued. "You have to be certified to build bridges, don't you? You need a license before you can drive. You need a teaching degree to teach. But raising a child? The most difficult and important job in the world? *For this,* you shouldn't need any qualifications?"

He'd heard all this before, but with the memory of Beatrice's devastating announcement fresh in his mind, something in the picture Karla presented didn't fit like it used to. It was the barest wisp of a feeling, but it made him uneasy.

"Okay, but did all men also harm their...y'know...?" He winced, unable to say the *w* word.

"Wives?" Karla smiled. "Of course not. Many men were kind to them—feeding them, protecting them, listening to them, and handling them with compassion. People treat their dogs the same way."

A vision of the ad from yesterday's billboard appeared. Should he tell Karla he was considering the operation? Becoming a woman? He opened his mouth but then closed it, unable to get the words out.

"Nick, get with the program. The institution of family is history." She paused. "There's the individual. There's the community. Nothing in between."

Nick fumbled with a Hershey's wrapper, trying to keep the candy bar from melting in his hand. He drew his knees toward his chest and took a deep breath.

"But sometimes...I feel empty." A small act of courage. Words he'd often wanted to say.

Karla's eyes narrowed. "You mean you're experiencing an *emotional void*, Nick? I'm astonished. Thanks to the Children's Centres, there are no more victims of marriage—kids exposed to constant vicious arguing. Kids bouncing between custody arrangements, with no real home. Kids unable to form trusting and meaningful relationships. We no longer have teenage pregnancies, latchkey kids, runaways." She raised her chin. "Thanks to the Children's Centres, you've been spared all that."

Nick didn't know what a latchkey kid was—or a runaway or a custody arrangement—but he grasped the basic point that family was bad. And yet, the thought that Karla might not have all the answers persisted like a shadow in the back of his mind. He'd have to continue wording his questions carefully, with deference. She was a friend but also a woman.

"But why are there people like Beatrice, with mental health—"

"They corrupt their minds with obscene literature and movies from the Age of Oppression, even though much of it is illegal—and frankly, even more ought to be." She leaned back, as if reconsidering. "Of course, that's not necessarily the situation with Beatrice."

"What do you mean?"

"Let's be frank, Nick. I think your friend has... motherhood syndrome."

Holy moly. He'd thought of such a possibility, but Karla had suggested it without even knowing about Beatrice's recent suicidal thoughts. All the more likely that Karla might be right.

Karla's expression softened. "Thankfully, we're making progress in treatment. In fact...I've been meaning to tell you, I've just been transferred to the mental health department in precisely that area."

"Uh congratulations," Nick mumbled, not sure if that was the proper response. She'd been transferred, not promoted.

"The best news is, I'll have a large budget and will probably be able to get you a *real* job."

Nick sighed. Performing magic allowed him to escape into a fantasy world. By transforming a king of clubs into a queen of hearts, he could change the impossible into the possible. By linking solid steel rings together, he could break through barriers that kept humans apart.

He had few opportunities to perform, though, and hated relying on handouts to make ends meet, like virtually every mankey he knew. Maybe an additional job wouldn't be a bad thing.

After Karla's face had faded from his screen, Nick licked the melted bits of Hershey's off his fingers. The hollow, empty feeling dissipated as he savoured them.

●

Karla turned off her phone, leaned back in her swivel chair and sighed. She stared at a drab puffer fish in her office mural.

Nick was the only mankey she cared about, the sole skeleton in her otherwise perfect closet. She'd known him as a small child, before they were both sent to the Children's Centre. Always talking, laughing, asking questions. Yes, *constantly asking questions.* Like breathing—he'd inhale an answer and exhale another question. But over the years he'd become increasingly dull. She attributed this to his lack of direction in life and possibly his sagging physique—like a puffer fish washed ashore.

As a little girl, Karla had enjoyed going to the park with Nico, as everyone called him then. The two of them would pull off their shoes and socks and run barefoot under the warm sun or play the silly ball games Nico invented. Although she was three years older, he had been big and smart, and she'd felt they were the same age.

Karla shook her head. All that seemed like a lifetime ago. She stared out her twentieth storey window at the darkening clouds.

She *could* cure Nick, restore him to his former self. She would persuade him to devote his life to the Movement, as she had chosen to do herself.

She fidgeted in her seat. His lack of enthusiasm—no, his *ambivalence*—with respect to the Movement's goals bothered her.

Karla sat up straight, then slammed an open hand down on her desk. *Dammit.* She hated ambivalence.

Severed Roots

Vacillation. Indecisiveness. They sapped one's energies, one's life force. She would purge Nick of those vices once and for all.

CHAPTER THREE

Late next morning, clutching his folded new umbrella, Nick stared at the globules of water rebounding off the windowpanes from his seat on the city bus. Beyond, the world was grey and gloomy.

He squinted. The blurry figure of a mankey, his bare head bobbing against the unrelenting torrent, scurried after a tall woman on the sidewalk while trying to keep an umbrella over her head.

Nick leaned back and closed his eyes, hoping to avert the throbbing pain growing in his right temple. He hated the smell of the damp seats, the nauseating vibrations from the engine, and the endless pounding of the raindrops.

And he wasn't looking forward to visiting Angelina, his old facilitator from the Children's Centre.

His eyes flicked open. *Maybe a diversion will help—I need this headache to subside.* He removed a playing card from his back pocket and held it up. In a flash, he slid the card over his ring and middle fingers with his thumb. His pinky and index finger guided the card smoothly. *Voilà,* it was hidden behind his hand. A quick reversal, and the card reappeared.

Nick scanned the other passengers. As expected, some of their melancholic faces came to life. They were watching his performance, albeit through sidelong glances on the part of the women. He grinned and sat up straighter. He continued to practice his sleight-of-hand trick, making the card appear and disappear in turn, the throbbing pain lessening with each flick of the card. Soon his thoughts drifted.

He hadn't seen Angelina in two months. How far had her cancer progressed? How was she coping? She must have been around seventy. That was a full life, right? Was she considering Dying with Dignity? Reducing the burden on society?

No, Angelina was not that altruistic.

Or maybe her old-fashioned views made her linger, made her cling on to life like a barnacle sticking to the bottom of a sinking boat. She had begun mentioning God and attending church, though she used to complain that religions changed with time to suit shifting societal beliefs and values.

Should he perform his card trick for her? Would it boost her spirits? Or just distract him from his discomfort at being in her presence? Why did she keep bugging him to visit her anyway? All these years! She was a woman, and he was a mankey.

Nick's thoughts shifted to Karla, the only other person in his life he had known since childhood. What had made them keep in touch into their thirties? He hadn't really made an effort, so it must have been Karla who desired the friendship.

He had no memory of how they'd met. The one time he'd asked her, years ago, she'd shrugged and replied that it wasn't important. An odd response. For *her* it wasn't important, but for him it obviously was, or he wouldn't have asked. Maybe it was time he asked her again.

A vision of Karla looming over Beatrice at the Women's Meeting made him squirm in his seat. Poor Beatrice. Her words haunted him.

"Do you know how I'm going to celebrate my birthday?"

Today was May 6. Beatrice's birthday was sometime in August. Was she serious about setting herself on fire? Did he have a right to interfere? She was a woman, after all. On the other hand, she respected his opinions. Maybe he could persuade her to seek counseling? His thoughts turned more rapidly than the queen of spades in his hand.

"Can you make an umbrella appear?" a male voice boomed from behind.

Nick's card flew from his hand. He bent down to catch it before it hit the wet floor. Turning as he stood up, he saw a slim, middle-aged man in the aisle. His face and neck were covered with so much hair, reddish and curly, he reminded Nick of a werewolf. The man was a full head shorter than Nick and sported a white collared shirt and green-and-orange checkered tie.

"Name's George." He extended his hand. "But you can call me Morrie—unless, of course, you like George better." He let out a cackling laugh, which triggered a loud, brassy, barking cough.

Nick took a step back, then reconsidered and stepped forward, not wanting to appear rude. The bus started moving again.

"Pardon me," the man wheezed, his extended hand suspended in the air. "I'm prone to catching pneumonia. Not the worst thing in the world, mind you, but a nuisance, nonetheless, particularly when you're trying to introduce yourself to a stranger. Doctor says it's chronic and viral, which means antibiotics are useless. She says I need plenty of rest, fluids, and most importantly, what I call 'dry living.'"

Nick reluctantly offered his hand, felt the man's bony but virile grip, and wondered whether he would catch something as a result of this unfortunate social protocol. "I'm Nick. Sorry to hear that."

"Bet you are. Listen, Nick. I saw you get on a few stops ago. You've been entertaining me ever since. I was wondering, do you live 'round here? You see, I left my umbrella at home. Didn't expect it to rain, much less this crazy downpour. In my delicate condition, getting even a *little* wet could be life-threatening."

Nick marvelled at how gregarious this diminutive man was. Regardless, he wasn't in the habit of sharing personal information with strangers. He squared his shoulders and tried to sound casual. "What does where I live have to do with you getting soaked?"

"Elementary, my friend. You're a young man—rather large, I must say—but presumably healthy. I was wondering if you could do me a *huge* favour and lend me your umbrella. I absolutely *must* get off at the next stop. You'll give me your address, of course, and first thing tomorrow morning I'll return the umbrella to you, along with my utmost and sincerest gratitude. You could be saving my life."

Nick was certain this character wouldn't bother to return his umbrella. On the other hand, other passengers were watching, waiting for his reaction. He had to display a modicum of graciousness. Besides, there was a peculiarity about this fellow—his air of authority, his self-confidence—that made it hard to deny his request.

Nick looked down at the umbrella propped against his empty seat: full-length, with a stainless-steel frame and a canopy made of a high-quality polyester fabric. Lately he'd been losing umbrellas, and yesterday, when he returned to the mall for the pink slippers, he'd had the brilliant idea of buying an expensive one to *force* himself not to lose it. He'd sacrificed a week's worth of Kraft dinners to acquire it.

Maybe he should step off the bus with the man and accompany him to his destination? No, he'd arrive late at Angelina's, and she'd suspect he wasn't crazy about visiting her. He didn't want to risk making her upset.

Mustn't show hesitation. People are watching. Nick made a quick, desperate search of the man's face for signs of sincerity and honesty but was unable to glean anything.

"I'm at 29 Blaire Road, in the basement apartment. Corner of Steinem," Nick mumbled, forfeiting a week's worth of nutrition to a total stranger.

"Thanks so much, Nick. It looks brand new. I'll try not to get it wet." Morrie ejected a staccato laugh, which morphed into a prolonged cough, as he glided to the exit, threw Nick a friendly salute and faded into the downpour.

Nick sighed. He fervently hoped the rain would die down by the time he needed to get off.

CHAPTER FOUR

Nick's clothes stuck to him like glue, even his underwear felt plastered on. He wished the Richmond Residence's lobby had a fireplace so he could dry off a little before he headed up to Angelina's suite. He was afraid of the elderly woman's reaction to his bedraggled appearance.

She would open the door and stare at him open-mouthed, taking in every detail. Then she would thrust a hand, palm up, inches from his nose and reprimand him for not using an umbrella, for neglecting his health. She'd treat him like an obtuse child who needed a lesson or two drilled into his head.

Nick shivered in front of the elevator, feeling the concierge's eyes on his back. He contemplated going out to buy a cheap umbrella, an umbrella he'd say the wind had broken, just so Angelina could see he had one. *No, that would be foolish and deceptive.* Though a master of magic, he loathed deception in real life.

Severed Roots

Surprisingly, giving away his umbrella brought a lightness to his shoulders, a rejuvenation of sorts. He really didn't mind giving it away after all.

He could tell her the truth, that he'd handed his umbrella to a complete stranger on the bus, to a mankey in need. *No, she'd think I was a liar. Or a fool.* Unless...the stranger was a woman? Mary, not Morrie. *Hmm.* In that case, Angelina might believe him.

But no, it's wrong to lie. Especially to a woman. A woman struck with cancer. After a few minutes of pacing back and forth and trying, idiotically, to shake off his wetness, he pressed the button to call the elevator.

On the seventh floor, Nick proceeded to door 703. He stood facing the small engraved letters: LENA CASTAGNA. *Hmm.* He'd never gotten around to asking Angelina why the nameplate said "Lena." He'd always known her as Angelina.

He knocked on her door.

Angelina took an unusually long time to respond. Finally, the heavy bolt clanked, then the door creaked open.

Nick gasped. She was thinner, her skin splotchy and dry, her hair wispy as though some of it had fallen out. Had it been only two months?

"I'm sorry," she said, huffing. "I find it difficult to walk across the room." She paused, the papery skin on her forehead creasing like an old dishrag. "Oh my God, look at you! You look worse than me!"

They settled in Angelina's dim living room, where she occupied a leather armchair and covered herself with a woolen blanket.

"This morning the nausea has been a little better," she said.

Nick sat three feet away on an adjacent sofa, wrapped in a thick, if rather small, white bathrobe. He cradled a mug of hot milk with honey. He appreciated that Angelina had prepared it for him, despite her illness, while he'd been in the shower.

"Time is precious." Angelina's voice shook. "I need to tell you what's on my mind. Keeping things inside makes the pain worse."

Nick held his breath. The soft oceanic sounds from a speaker near the ceiling did little to ease his anxiety.

Angelina picked up a ring of fresh pineapple from the plate on the coffee table and held it between her thin fingers, before sucking and nibbling around its perimeter with intense resolve.

"Nick," she finally said, "I always enjoy your company. You're a good listener, even though you may not be a great talker. And these days I really need someone who will listen to me."

"So do I."

Angelina frowned, and Nick immediately regretted his reply.

Nick switched his gaze to the flowerpots hanging from the ceiling behind Angelina. The living room was sparse, the usual clutter gone.

"Now...Nick..."

His focus snapped back to Angelina.

"The cancer has spread to my bones and liver."

Nick swallowed. A few words, a new reality. For years, an inexplicable sense of duty had made Nick bus across town several times a year to visit her—usually, though, only after she phoned to nag him about how *happy* she'd be to see him. As much as Nick hated these visits, often guiltily finding himself pining for the day Angelina's illness would overcome her, now that it was happening, a strange lump formed in the back of his throat.

"Oh, my gosh," he said.

"The doctor said there's no point in further treatment, and recommended an injection. Quick and painless." Her voice was flat, her eyes distant. She seemed to be looking *through* him.

"I said no thanks, I don't 'do' dying until I have to." So they're moving me into Franklin House, in Grace

Hospital—in fact, not far from your home. I should be there for...three to eight weeks." She might as well have been speaking of someone else. There was no emotion in her voice.

Nick stirred more honey from the jar on the coffee table into his milk. Three to eight weeks? How long had he known her? Twenty years? Twenty-five? He must have been about eight or nine when she started caring for him at the Children's Centre.

And now, only another three to eight weeks? *Hmm*...that meant...based on his past schedule...only one or two more face-to-face encounters. Or would she expect more visits? Did dying bring greater entitlement? Nick chided himself for entertaining these awful thoughts. Then he shuddered. *Am I incapable of any human compassion?*

For a long time, Angelina sat still. The breeze from the open patio caressed Nick's face.

Without warning, her eyes widened, and her head swayed from side to side. She rose to a half-standing position and gripped Nick's hand.

"Nick, I don't want to die among strangers!"

Her skeletal fingers sent a tremor down Nick's spine. Death had touched him. Nick willed time to move faster.

Angelina slumped back, her knees unable to support her in the stooped position. "I'm told in the final three or four days, I can expect to stop eating and drinking, struggle to breathe, and feel like I'm on an emotional roller coaster—angry, sad, happy, frightened, delirious. They reassured me the nursing staff will be at my bedside during the last hours. Hell, I don't even know their names."

Nick bit at his lip. He needed to say something. He recalled Angelina's recent interest in religion.

"Is there a chaplain?"

"Damn the chaplain!" Angelina slammed her hands down on the arms of her chair. "A nurse told me the chaplain regularly calls in sick; claims being around dying people makes her depressed."

Angelina's blanket began to slide down her back. She yanked it onto her right shoulder, then reached for her mug with a trembling hand and took a sip. After putting it down, she shut her eyes and appeared to be drifting off. Suddenly, she opened them and leaned forward.

"Nick, I can't give you any money this time. I need every penny for my medications."

Nick shrugged, wanting to preserve his dignity. "Thanks. I'm managing. I've been called to do a show at Goldilocks in two weeks, which hopefully—"

"I wish I could come." She lifted her chin. "I always enjoy watching your performances."

Was that a gleam in her eye? Angelina was a big fan, and he appreciated that.

Angelina picked up a framed photograph from the coffee table.

"I've been studying this photo a lot lately. Did I ever tell you my parents were old-fashioned Italians, devout Catholics? When they met, my father wanted to buy a house, get married, have children." She paused.

"Soon after the wedding, though—or so my mother told me—he walloped her across the side of the head with the flat of his hand. This continued over the years, whenever he had too much to drink."

Angelina shifted her weight on the armchair and let out a string of weak coughs.

"My sister and I lived through his yelling, his insults, his threats against our mother. Thankfully, it wasn't like that every day, and we also had happy times as a family."

Her voice deepened. "But my father believed he had a right to control every aspect of my mother's life—what she wore, how she spent their money, who she socialized with—and he would lash out whenever his authority was challenged."

Angelina replaced the photo frame on the coffee table and sucked on another ring of pineapple. Juice slid down her chin, leaving a wet trail faintly visible in the muted light.

"I never told you this," Angelina continued. "When I came of age, my parents expected me to get married."

Nick grimaced.

"Insane, isn't it? No one I knew—except my sister—was getting married anymore. People had lost interest. Women had surpassed men in education, income, social standing...everything. We were bringing them shame. And this was even before B&S."

Nick had learned about B&S, a radical offshoot of the third-wave Me Too movement. Controversial at first, the Blame & Shame campaign was a game changer. Many men, following the example of the Five Celebrities, started taking testosterone suppressants and the newest antilibidinal drugs, desperate to gain back some self-respect and public acceptance.

Angelina snorted. "But my father didn't give a hoot what the rest of the world thought or did. 'Herd mentality is for cattle,' he'd say. Shaking a finger at me day after day in his sweaty undershirt, he tormented me until I gave in. Then, ignoring the sneers and taunts of our neighbours, he set me up with Alberto—another dinosaur stuck in the past. I was only twenty-nine."

Was she going to wipe the juice off her chin? Should he offer to bring her a tissue from the bathroom? Or would that embarrass her by calling attention to her appearance? Nick wished he knew the right thing to do.

"Wasn't marriage illegal?" he asked.

Angelina shook her head. "The whole thing was being hotly debated. God, those endless public consultations…"

Angelina dug inside her blanket and muttered something about the heating pad. "Anyways, shortly after our little Billy turned two, there was a knock on our door. It was a marriage counselor. Marriage counselors were government officials, abrasive women in their twenties sent to encourage any married couples that were still left to end their marriages."

Nick nodded slowly, as an ache formed in his chest. In all these years, he'd never known Angelina was a marriage survivor. It explained why she had seldom spoken about her past.

"Well, Alberto refused to talk to her. She tried to cajole us, then threatened us with a bogus fine. It didn't work. A few days after the Marriage Abolition Act came into force, the police arrested Alberto. Women weren't normally taken away, only mankeys. I never heard from him again."

Angelina leaned forward, her sunken eyes wide open.

"Things got even worse once a new Advisor was elected. More Children's Centres opened, and I received the dreaded notice: they were going to 'liberate' Billy." She wrung her hands.

Nick stared down into his mug. He wished he could relate to Angelina's experiences.

"I wanted to hide him, to run away with him, but I knew I'd be caught and thrown in jail. As Billy and I sat on the bus bound for the Centre, he cried, and the more I tried to comfort him, the more hysterical he became. He was only seven. After we arrived, I had to tear myself away. I left him bawling his eyes out in the arms of total strangers."

She took a deep breath, shut her eyes, and exhaled slowly. "They didn't tell me he was dead until after the funeral."

Nick raised his eyebrows. Angelina opened her eyes.

"After Billy was cremated, I discovered he had slipped a note deep into my purse during my one and only visit." Her face contorted. "It was a suicide note, Nick. It read: *This life hurts without you, Mommy. I want to sleep forever.—Billy.*"

Angelina put down her mug and readjusted her blanket.

"I stopped eating. I gave up bathing. I forgot how to laugh. Eventually, I pulled myself together and applied for a job at a Children's Centre. I wanted to understand what kind of environment could lead a child—my son—to take his life. I hoped I could push for reforms. That's when we met, Nico." She smiled faintly. "You were one of my first pupils."

She'd always called him Nico. That was his real name, what they'd called him at the Centre. He didn't remember his last name, but he'd known it was Italian. He'd been only five or six when he'd entered the place. One morning, the director of the centre had all the kids line up in front of her, and one by one she'd assigned each a different surname—"as different as possible from your parents'," she'd explained. His new last name would be Wong. This was one of the most popular surnames in the world, the director later told him. He should feel lucky to have that name.

Nick swallowed. "Seems like I've known you forever."

"I've always been fond of you, Nico. Maybe because you were close to Billy's age. Or because we both have an Italian background. Or..." She lowered her head.

Nick squirmed in his seat. Angelina's bathrobe felt uncomfortably tight around his shoulders. He wanted to take it off. After all, he was fully dry now and no longer needed it. He started undoing the belt and stopped. *Will Angelina mind? Maybe she'll criticize my eating habits when she sees all the flab on my body. No, better leave the robe on.*

He glanced at his watch and leaned forward, wondering whether it was better manners for one to announce their intention to leave and then get up or get up first and then make the announcement.

"There's something else," Angelina said, signaling with her hand for him to stay put.

"What is it?"

Angelina tilted her head in a side-to-side rhythm. Her mouth was open, but words wouldn't come out.

"Let's leave it for next time," she finally said, her voice barely audible. "I'm tired. Dying is hard work."

Nick was relieved to escape Angelina's apartment, but his heart ached.

The rain had abated by the time he headed to the bus stop. His sweatshirt and blue cotton pants felt damp even after a tumble through Angelina's dryer.

What had he accomplished? She hadn't been able to give him money this time. He hadn't offered her any comforting words. He had merely been there. And while he was very interested in hearing her talk about the Children's Centre, he wished he knew, in all these years, how he was supposed to relate to this elderly woman. She was no longer his facilitator, so what was the purpose of their relationship?

Nick looked down at the dark, wet pavement.

Now she expects me to visit her at Franklin House, and I'll probably end up going. Not because I want to, but because...

He gazed at one of his sneakers, following the path of the white lace as it crisscrossed the eyelets.

Maybe there isn't any reason. Maybe visiting someone you know on their deathbed is something we're supposed to do as humans.

Seated on the bus, Nick's thoughts shifted to Angelina's parents. What would make them—or any married couple, for that matter—want to stay together, to *live together*? The two were so different: one was a mankey, the other, a woman.

Nick shook his head. Aloneness was best, his facilitators had often said. Sharing your life with others diluted your individuality. Besides, they said that the people closest to you always caused the deepest hurt.

But if that was obvious, why hadn't people always thought like that?

Nick examined the tattoo on the back of his hand, the orange circle overlapping the black one. He wondered for the hundredth time what it had been like in the past—to be wild, to be a savage. He'd once heard men—they were always called men then, not mankeys—would fantasize about sex on average five to twenty times a day. How could they live like that? How could they go about their daily activities tormented by powerful urges, slaves to their hormones? It must have been constant torture.

He slid a finger over the number imprinted below the orange and black circles: 5858-12-5. The number indicated the clinic and age of the boy when the mandatory chemical injection, referred to as the Rite of Passage, had been administered. Most boys had it done around twelve years of age. His treatment had been at twelve and a half—exactly twenty years ago.

Notwithstanding the severe consequences of noncompliance, including surgical castration, few boys attempted to dodge the Rite of Passage because the benefit was obvious: complete elimination of sexual hunger.

Boys were required to return to the clinic every six months thereafter for monitoring, until they reached the age of twenty-five. Some circumvented all this by choosing gender reassignment surgery instead. This was considered the ideal option, an admirable act, but it was not for everyone. In any case, the government allowed people the choice.

5858-12-5. An atonement for thousands of years of abusing women and children. A social responsibility. Freedom from obsession with sex and self-centredness.

Freedom to build a safer world.

CHAPTER FIVE

Nick lingered at the Mankey Bar entrance. He soaked in the faint Baroque music, the jangle of voices drifting from the dark corners of the pub, and the scent of fries and mulled apple juice. He was thankful for the music. The intricate melodies stirred a longing for something wholesome he couldn't identify.

Miles waved from across the bar. "Hey, the magician's here."

Instinctively, Nick patted his front pants pockets, then his back. He inhaled sharply. *Ape brain*. He must have left his playing cards at Angelina's when he used her clothes dryer.

Nick sighed. Magic always cheered him up, and after his meeting with Angelina earlier today, he could certainly use some cheering up.

He checked his watch: 8:45 p.m. He couldn't turn around and go home—Miles had seen him. Thankfully, the pub closed at ten. He'd heard the place used to stay open much later back in the horrid days when pubs were loud and crowded. Back then, women also frequented them; fistfights were common and alcohol flowed freely.

Still, for the next hour and fifteen minutes he'd be stuck, a mere audience for his friends as they droned on, instead of a performer of magic. He'd be sitting at a sticky table, listening to Miles extol his landlady's plumbing skills. Simon would probably go on about his usual social anxieties. He'd have to sit through Derek whining about not getting the garbage-mankey job he'd been vying for. Worst of all, Spindley would be trying to convince everyone his insomnia was his body's defence mechanism against nerdy aliens plotting to seize control of his brain.

Maybe Nick should talk about his own problems for once. Solicit his friends' advice on how he could help Beatrice? But no. Mankeys weren't supposed to have close female friends; his buddies, especially Miles and Simon, would find Nick weird.

Sighing, Nick ambled across the dimly lit room, past the rows of scruffy looking mankeys who always drank alone, to the far wall adorned with mounts that once, he'd heard, held animal heads. Seated at the table were only three of his pals. "Where's Derek? He hasn't been here in a while."

"Must've gotten tired of us," said Spindley, yawning. "I don't blame him. He's a bright fella."

Simon looked up from his glass of tomato juice. "My guess is he did the switch. It's what he'd been talking 'bout last time he was here, 'member? Said he'd become a woman and land himself a good job."

"Takes guts." Nick plopped down in his usual seat while reaching for the bowl of peanuts near Simon's elbow. He recalled the billboard ad he'd seen the other day and how he'd considered undergoing the operation himself.

"Whatever," said Miles. "The only one here who's got a job is Nick. Betcha he's a woman in disguise."

The others chuckled.

"It's a woman's world," Nick said, trying to deflect the focus away from himself. "We had our turn for thousands of years and blew it."

"And we finally got peace." Spindley threw a peanut into his mouth. "No wars for...how many years now?"

"Yeah, just the rioting," Nick said.

"Getting worse," Miles chimed in.

The waiter—a lean, fidgety mankey in a white collared shirt, who had probably recently graduated from Children's Centre—had positioned himself a few feet away. Nick signaled to him and ordered a glass of Coke. Not that Nick needed a sugar or caffeine boost at this hour, but ordering a drink was expected in a pub. Besides, it would provide him with a whole suite of activities to engage in when the conversation became tiresome: He could reach for the glass, cradle it, slide it a few inches back and forth along the tabletop, sip from it, swish the liquid inside, stare at it, look up from it.

Miles turned to Nick. "So, you gonna show us a new trick?"

Nick rubbed the back of his neck. "Can't. Don't have my cards with me."

"What?" Spindley shifted in his seat. "You can't do this to us."

"Sorry. I forgot them. I'll show you guys some tricks next time."

Spindley raised his voice. "Look, I'm tired of your carelessness."

Nick's body tensed. Miles and Simon straightened.

Spindley glared at Nick for a few seconds, then looked away. "Ahh, forget it. I'm just cranky."

"What's the matter, Spin?" asked Miles.

Spindley folded his skinny arms across his chest and looked down at the table, appearing to study the bumps in the paint. "Last night, while I lay in bed, three of those troublemakers I've been tellin' you about— y'know, with the pink-crystal faces—knocked on my skull repeatedly and begged to be let inside. *Begged* me. At first, I was surprised 'cause they're usually not so insistent. But then I got the sense they were desperate, and I started feelin' sorry for them..."

Miles, Simon, and Nick exchanged furtive glances, as if to say, *Someone better change the subject fast, or we're in for a long, painful rest of the evening.*

Nick leaned forward. "Their faces were pink, you said?"

Spindley nodded. "Their hair, too."

"Interesting," said Nick.

"Why's that?" Spindley asked.

"Well, 'cause tomorrow's Memorial Day. Y'know, pink slippers and all." He kicked Miles under the table.

"Oh, yeah." Miles slapped his forehead with exaggerated motion. "Memorial Day. Luckily I still have my slippers from last year."

Simon shrugged. "I don't have no pink slippers. Can't afford 'em. But don't matter to me, as I plan on stayin' inside the whole day anyway, like I done every year."

Miles, Simon, and Spindley sipped their drinks. Nick scooped up more peanuts while impatiently waiting for his Coke to arrive.

After a long silence, Miles spoke. "Think the riots will lead to civil war?"

"Better not," said Nick. "We can't afford to lose lives. I heard the world population is shrinking almost 7 percent a year."

Miles snorted. "I'm not surprised. Not enough surrogates keen on having their bodies invaded for nine months at a time. No matter what the pay."

Severed Roots

"Yup." Spindley raised a mark-my-words finger in the air. "And as soon as the human pop has shrunk to a few million, with mostly old folk and no one to care for 'em, the aliens are gonna take over the planet."

Nick leaned back while the waiter placed a tall glass of Coke in front of him. He took a sip from the straw. Then another.

They all sipped their drinks.

"Forget the human population," Nick finally said, breaking the silence. He was afraid he'd finish his drink too soon if he didn't start talking. "The mankey population is nose-diving even faster."

Miles rolled his eyes. "That's 'cause the Advisor *wants* it that way. It's obviously good for the world if the Advisor wants it, right?"

"Makes sense," Simon said. "We elected her."

Spindley leaned in, an offensive, onion-like smell emanating from his body. "You can look at it as a social evolution thingy. Ever hear of the black widow spider? She eats her mate once he's no longer useful to her."

Everyone cringed.

A thought occurred to Nick, and he slapped his hand on the table. "Listen guys. Just because we elected the Advisor, doesn't mean she's right in everything. We elected the least bad candidate—or at least I know I did."

Miles looked toward the ceiling and whistled. "Heavy thinking, dude. But the Advisor's a woman, and we're mankeys. So it would be perentious—pretension—to say we know better. You need to trust our leaders, Nick."

Hmm. Trust our leaders? How much blood was shed throughout history because people blindly followed their leaders?

"Pretentious," said Nick in a controlled tone. "The word is *pretentious*."

Miles scowled at Nick.

Everyone fell silent again, and then, in unison, each mankey took another sip.

"Faccia da culo!"

Nick looked up from his glass as a beast of a mankey in a yellow tank top too small for his size yelled and pounded his fist on the table a few feet away.

Everyone froze. The guy leaned over, biceps bulging, and grabbed the collar of a scrawny, bespectacled young mankey across from him with his left hand, while bringing his right fist back, appearing to take aim.

Nick jumped up, surprising himself. "Wait!" He scurried over.

Muscleman twisted his broad shoulders toward Nick. "Mind-a your own business," he said, his eyes hard. "Or I'm-a gonna knock you too."

Legs shaking, Nick forced himself to take a step closer. He couldn't bear to witness violence, least of all a bloody face. "I'm Italian, like you...although I don't speak the language. I want to know what this guy did to make you so angry."

Muscleman glared at Nick for a long time. Then, slowly, he lowered his right arm while maintaining his hold on scrawny man's collar.

"*Eh*. I come-a looking for a chair. Dis *gentleman-key* drink alone, so I ask politely, 'Please, can I take dis odder chair?' And he say to my face, 'No problemo, Mussolini.'"

Nick's mouth fell open.

The pallid-faced mankey's terror-stricken eyes darted in all directions.

"Why did you call him Mussolini?" Nick asked.

"Because he's a *faccia da culo*," intervened muscleman, fisting his right hand again. "He no like Italians."

Nick stood tall, gaining confidence that he could control the situation. "Listen, *amico*. Please let the fellow talk. I'm sure there's a good explanation."

Muscleman grunted and released his grip on scrawny man's collar.

Scrawny man sucked in a few quick breaths. "I-I said it in jest. I-I've never seen a mankey with that kind of body. So I called him 'mussolini.' Doesn't that mean 'muscular' in Italian?"

Nick suppressed a chuckle. Muscleman's eyes softened.

"Mussolini is the name of an evil person," said Nick. "I think he was a leader in Italy during the Age of Oppression and he...despised democracy."

"I'm s-so s-sorry," scrawny man said, laying a shaky hand against his breastbone. "I didn't know..."

Nick nodded to muscleman. "See, amico? It's good to investigate. I'm a magician. Things are not always what they seem."

Muscleman muttered something in Italian and turned to scrawny man. "It's *muscoloso*. I am muscoloso. Next time, don't-a use words you don't-a know what they say." He lifted the unoccupied chair with one hand and strutted away.

Nick smiled and took a long breath before rejoining his buddies.

"Good stuff," Miles said.

"Good stuff," echoed Simon.

"Way to go," mumbled Spindley. "Though, to be honest, I wouldn't have minded seeing a little more...y'know...action."

When Nick arrived home, he pushed his front door closed harder than necessary, his bones leaden with exhaustion. He ran a hand through his hair. *What a rotten, wasted evening. Sitting around my reeking friends, listening to their inane remarks. Consuming three overpriced Cokes I didn't even want. Busing for two hours for that!*

Oh, and that hotheaded muscleman—why can't people solve issues peacefully?

In all the years he'd been going there, Nick had never seen a physical fight in the Mankey Bar. Or anywhere else for that matter, except skirmishes instigated by Hardinians on the news. Unlike in the Age of Oppression, when fistfights, stabbings, and shootings were normal expressions of male culture, mankeys today rarely fought. It was something he was grateful for.

Nick lifted two solid metal rings off the floor and gazed at their perfect circular shapes. Deftly, he passed one ring through the other, linking them. Immediately, some of the tension in his neck and shoulders melted away, as if by magic.

After fiddling for an hour with other props, he yawned, changed and settled down onto the floor mattress.

He felt cold under his thick blanket.

He pictured Beatrice, her genuine, wide smile framed by shoulder-length golden hair. She was probably the only person he enjoyed talking to. Why didn't he spend more time with her? He wished he could, but social norms obliged him to hold back. And what had possessed him to behave so callously toward her at Amazon Mall? Ugh! He needed to apologize. Was she serious about setting herself on fire in front of the Ministry building on her birthday? What could he do to stop her?

It took him a long time to fall asleep.

CHAPTER SIX

Beatrice **banged incessantly** on Nick's door, but no matter how hard he tried to pull the door open for her, he was unable to. Women in navy blue suits were pulling at the handle on the other side. Nick's armpits dripped sweat. He had only a few more seconds to pry the door open before Beatrice gave up knocking and left for the Ministry building in order to...God, no! Nick tried to shout. He opened his mouth to scream, but no sound came out. Having succeeded in turning the handle, he pulled on it manically until his arms burned and he could no longer breathe. Suddenly in a moment of clarity, he was yanked into cold, hard reality.

Opening his eyes, he breathed a deep sigh of relief. *Beatrice is safe.*

The knocking continued. With a grunt, he tore himself out of bed and headed toward the dilapidated front door of his basement apartment in his boxer shorts, stumbling through the magic props littering the floor. He yelped in pain as he stepped on a thimble set, then kicked a tennis ball and a metal ring out of the way before skidding on an instruction manual.

Nick opened the door and squinted at a slim, thickly bearded figure that looked vaguely familiar.

"What a marvelous morning," the visitor said, thrusting a neatly folded umbrella into Nick's hands. "It's amazing how the weather changes from one day to the next. But geez, how about that rain yesterday? I've never seen such a deluge. Did you manage to stay dry?"

That nut from the bus. What was his name? Morrie! "What time is it?"

"Five-thirty. So sorry. I would've come earlier, but nobody answered the main door when I rang. I thought I had the wrong address and walked up and down the block like a moron. Forgot you lived in a hole in the ground."

Nick yawned. "Five-thirty *in the morning?*"

"What, you want it to be five-thirty in the afternoon? Of course, it's the morning. It's the start of a special day."

Nick thought for a moment and remembered. It was Age of Oppression Memorial Day. Everyone was expected to forgo eating in the morning as a collective expression of grief. At noon, a siren would sound in thousands of cities, towns and villages, signaling the end of the fast. People would stop their activities and stand at attention for a minute of silence for the victims of male oppression. He used to do all that, although less so in recent years. Still, it was the most solemn day on the calendar, and Morrie sounded cheerful about it.

Nick decided to play dumb. "It is?"

"You mean you don't know? Are you for real?"

Nick didn't respond.

"Why, it's the first Tuesday of the week."

Nick raised an eyebrow. "Um…there's only one Tuesday in the week."

"That makes it even more special. Think about it. There's only one Tuesday in the week, and it happens to be today!"

"Well," said Nick with a grin. "There's also only one Wednesday in the week and only one Thursday and—"

"That means each day is special!"

Nick smirked. "So, I guess we should be celebrating?"

"You got it." Morrie pushed his way into the apartment. He opened his duffel bag and pulled out a long bottle and two wine glasses. "Château Carbonnieux's 1996 Bordeaux. A *tra-dee-sionnel* red blend of Cabernet Sauvignon, Merlot, and Cabernet Franc." He carefully twisted the protruding cork and jerked it out.

Nick stared at Morrie, assuming this odd gesture was Morrie's way of saying thank you for saving him from pneumonia.

"I don't drink. Certainly not at this hour."

"*C'est la folie!*" Morrie filled a glass and handed it to Nick. He poured another glass for himself. "To our health," he bellowed and downed it in one gulp.

Nick looked at his glass. He didn't know if he should; the facilitators at the Children's Centre had insisted drinking alcohol and smoking weed were unsafe for mankeys, but…w*hat the heck.* He raised it to his lips, letting the fruity aroma fill his nostrils, and took a slow sip. A bitter taste tingled his palate. His face warmed. This was a special day, after all. A complete stranger he'd helped on the bus had returned his umbrella. He should mark the moment.

"Your card trick was impressive," Morrie said. His gaze fell on a magic-instruction manual by his feet, its front cover partially torn off. "Are you a professional magician?"

For some reason, Nick didn't want his visitor to know he frequently relied on welfare, even though most mankeys lived that way. "It's my passion."

Morrie refilled both glasses. "To your talent and prosperity!" He downed the contents of his glass.

Nick grimaced and followed suit. *A mankey drinking so much alcohol…*

"Do you teach?" Morrie asked, putting away the wine bottle. "I'd like to take lessons."

Nick coughed as the wine burned his throat. "Why d'you wanna learn magic?"

Morrie strode to the only chair in the living room, almost tripping over the floor mattress, and banged into the green hybrid bike leaning against the wall. He sat and placed his empty glass on the dusty hardwood floor. He crossed his legs, linked his fingers behind his head and inhaled. Sunlight streamed in through the window, conjuring up a column of dust particles above his lap.

"Magic," Morrie began, lifting his chin and looking down his nose at Nick, "keeps us alive by taking our breath away." With a laugh, he relaxed his posture.

Nick smiled.

Morrie's laugh had morphed into a grin so wide it created deep furrows in his cheeks and around his eyes. "It takes you into a world where the impossible is made possible." He clapped his hands. "Magic always fascinated me as a child. Transports me back to preschool, when *everything* was magical, when seeing a crayon spread colour onto a page was astounding."

Nick nodded, delighted. Despite his quirky manners, Morrie was genial and seemed to share Nick's passion. He decided he'd be happy to give his visitor lessons. Besides, he could use the money to acquire a few nifty magic props he'd been eyeing lately.

"So, how about a couple of hours in the afternoon?" said Nick. "Mondays and Fridays? My fee is minimum wage. We'll cover card tricks, rope, sponge balls—beginner stuff like that. And later—well, maybe even mind reading using a hidden microcamera."

"Deal." Morrie retrieved the bottle from his bag and refilled both their glasses. "To my apprenticeship!"

"I've had enough," said Nick, pointing to the wine bottle.

"What? Why?"

"Why? Uh...why not? Get it? *Wine not!* Ha!"

Morrie chuckled. After emptying his glass, he sprang from his seat. "Tell me, my friend. Since I'm already here, how about giving me my first lesson right now?"

A smile crept across Nick's face. Although it was Memorial Day and he had considered attending the local ceremony, he never liked the crowds, the noise, the long-winded speeches.

Nick quickly pulled a pair of sweatpants over his boxer shorts and took out a deck of cards. His excitement about teaching Morrie overpowered his craving for sleep or food.

Throughout the lesson, Morrie impressed him as a diligent student. Although probably in his late forties, he moved and talked like an eager teenager. After three hours, he asked whether there was anything to eat.

Eat? It was only midmorning. Maybe Morrie didn't know it was Memorial Day. No, that couldn't be—he seemed too astute not to know these things. As he glanced down, it struck Nick that Morrie was not wearing the obligatory pink slippers. He had risked coming to Nick's apartment in black running shoes! True, few people were on the street at five-thirty in the morning and it was dark, but how would Morrie get back home undetected? *He must have his pink slippers in his duffel bag.*

"I guess you don't fast on Memorial Day morning?" Nick asked in his most casual voice.

"A day to commemorate the evils of the past is fine." Morrie reached conspicuously for his Bordeaux. "But not the evilness of desire." He refilled his glass and raised it to his lips.

"Evilness of desire…?"

Morrie lowered his glass without drinking. "Nick, I'll give you an example. Women have been abused and hurt because of men's bodily urges. But that's never been the fault of the urge, only the failure of men to control it."

Interesting. Nick had been taught that removal of the male sex drive was the last hope humans had as a species. For decades, society tried hard to dismantle toxic masculinity…sexism…misogyny…male privilege…even gender differences. In the end, it all failed. How could Morrie be so unorthodox in his views?

"But," said Nick, "hasn't history proven men are incapable of controlling their urges? Even when *religions* taught restraint, that didn't—"

"Religions focused too much on God and not enough on godliness—the godliness inherent in every human being, the godliness that engenders respect for others. This"—Morrie held up the tattooed back of his right hand—"is a disgrace to our humanity."

Nick's breath hitched. He'd never heard a mankey refer to the Rite of Passage in such a degrading way.

His stomach grumbled, reminding him he'd been up insanely early that morning and had worked hard. Perhaps he deserved to eat, even though it was Memorial Day morning. Entering the tiny kitchen in the corner of his apartment, Nick glanced at the window, reassuring himself no one could look in through the thick curtain.

"Okay, I'll make us some fried eggs and toast." Nick threw some bread in the toaster and, after selecting the pan that looked the least greasy, fried a half dozen eggs on the stove top. Morrie and Nick seated themselves on wooden stools and chatted about magic over breakfast.

"I look forward to working with the microcamera," Morrie said later, standing by the door. "When you're ready to teach me, that is." He paid Nick for his lesson, gave him a friendly salute and let himself out.

Nick sauntered to his mattress, sat down and stretched his legs. A few minutes later he realized with a jolt that Morrie had not changed into pink slippers. If caught by the police, he could receive a steep fine. Memorial Day, despite Morrie's nonchalance, was not to be taken lightly.

Nick stared at the eclipse tattoo on the back of his hand. A disgrace to our humanity? *That's what the black circle represents,* Nick imagined Karla replying if he were to ask her. And the orange circle? *That represents a brighter world, of course,* she'd say with a sympathetic smile. *Your new acquaintance talked about godliness? Yes, but we can't legislate godliness, Nick, can we?* Or something like that. Karla had an answer for everything.

But Morrie had stirred unease within him, and he wanted to understand why. Nick needed things in his life to make sense. He recalled an aphorism Beatrice had once shared with him: "Truth is a friend that never betrays."

He ambled to the fridge, opened a can of pop, and glanced at the digital wall clock. It was only ten fifteen. There was still time to attend the local Memorial Day ceremony. Maybe he'd learn something new. Besides, no one there would know he hadn't fasted. Or would they?

He quickly poured the cold liquid down his throat.

CHAPTER SEVEN

Nick pushed through the crowd to get close to the makeshift stage in front of the Peace Tower on Parliament Hill. A large white screen loomed overhead on which this year's Memorial Day ceremonies would soon play out.

It had been three years since he'd attended a Memorial Day event. The memory of mankeys stepping up to the lectern—mankeys of different ages, different ethnicities—filled his mind. Beneath the big banners, amid solemn music and chants of "Our future is near," each mankey had spoken for one or two minutes. They begged forgiveness from all women and children, dead and living, for the immeasurable evils patriarchy had perpetrated on them over the centuries. Nick's cheeks had burned while listening to some of those apologies, and he'd wished he could fade into nothingness.

In the past, he'd looked for a seat far from the stage, seeing his attendance solely as a moral obligation.

But this time, spurred by a deepening curiosity, he wanted to be closer.

Nick found a spot on the manicured lawn, sat and extended his legs on the cool grass, careful not to brush them against anyone nearby, most of whom were women. His bulky thighs prevented him from sitting cross-legged, and for a minute, he gazed at the pink slippers encasing his feet. *Hmm*. Had Morrie been caught and fined for wearing black running shoes on Memorial Day? He hoped not. Although...maybe Morrie *wanted* to be caught? A personal protest? How could free countries like Canada impose such a footwear requirement on mankeys, even if it was only one day a year? He'd read that in the US and a few other countries, the Pink Slippers Law was being challenged in the courts.

Behind the stage, the Peace Tower soared ninety meters, a magnificent sandstone structure with tall Gothic lines and a huge clock in the centre. Atop the tower Canada's flag billowed. Each corner was adorned with a red maple leaf, while the centre of the flag displayed a solid orange circle eclipsing a solid black circle.

Nick liked being on these grounds. The Parliament buildings with their rough stone walls, multiple entrances and sculptured roof lines evoked a feeling of a majestic bygone era. One he wished he knew better.

Nego Huzcotoq

The crowd thickened around him. Two women with grey, cotton-candy hair down to their hips stood in a side hug smoking weed, periodically waving a joint over their heads, inviting "any lady here" to take a hit.

Recorded coverage of the Age of Oppression Memorial Day events appeared on the giant screen. People who were still standing sat down wherever they could find a patch of grass.

The international committee had decided that this year the main ceremony would take place at the Colosseum in Rome. The Advisor, flanked by three women on each side, approached the lectern. She looked erect and regal on the screen, with a wizened face and flowing white hair.

"Our future is near!" she said to thunderous applause. "*Il nostro futuro è vicino!*

"Two thousand years ago, this immense amphitheatre was packed, much as it is today. But for a very different reason." Her high-pitched, forceful voice grated on Nick's nerves. "Surrounded by these great arches, tens of thousands of citizens gathered regularly to watch gladiators fight wild beasts—and even people—for entertainment. It was a place of blood, gore and screaming spectators." Her right cheek twitched as she spoke. The top strands of her hair danced in the breeze.

"My friends, over the centuries this desire to subjugate has taken on myriad forms and expressions. You are well aware of the dismal history of our species. In light of the systemic oppression, repression and subjugation of women and children by mankeys since the dawn of civilization, we are assembled today not only to reflect on our past but, more importantly, to reaffirm our commitment to the ultimate goal of our movement—*heaven on earth.*"

Wild applause erupted on the screen and all around Nick, along with chants of "Our future is near." Nick squirmed. Didn't every movement in history aim to create heaven on earth? And didn't every movement fail? He joined in the applause half-heartedly.

"It is hard to believe," the Advisor continued, "that until a few decades ago, most people in the world were sanguists."

Sanguism. Loyalty based on blood. One facilitator at the Children's Centre had called it the longest-standing blemish on human history.

"Let me share a tale with you from the dark Age of Oppression. This fellow, Stephen, was aloof toward his coworker Matthew. Stephen never invited Matthew to dinner or any of his celebrations. It was not out of malice but simply because they had different personalities and interests.

"Well, one day, Stephen learned by accident that Matthew was his cousin. Suddenly, their relationship changed. Matthew was now invited and *expected* to attend Stephen's family celebrations. Yet nothing had changed between them except for the simple knowledge they had a common ancestor, whom neither of them even knew.

"My friends, is there anything more irrational?"

The bar graph at the bottom corner of the screen shifted. The popular approval rating for the Advisor across the World Federation now hovered at 77 percent. Her highest ratings were in Sweden and Denmark—91 percent each—followed by Canada at 87 percent. The US was the lowest, at 63 percent.

"But sanguism is not the worst evil." The Advisor paused and steepled her thin fingers. The image on the screen zoomed in on a group of women and mankeys huddled together, standing motionless under the great stone arches of the Colosseum, soaking up the Advisor's every word and gesture.

"There was an organization called the Children's Aid Society. It operated in every major city..."

Nick's neck muscles ached. He had been up since five-thirty. He rotated his head and batted his eyelids to keep himself alert.

"...and it was an abject failure. The number of child abuse cases kept rising—alcoholic fathers who beat their children, crack-addicted mothers..."

Nick looked up at the slow-moving white clouds.

"Why did this organization fail?" The Advisor's voice became more strained, almost pleading. "It was not due to a lack of resolve. It was not due to a lack of funding. It failed because it tried to prevent child abuse by *embracing, strengthening,* and *supporting families*—the very institution that led to the abuses in the first place."

The harsh tone of the Advisor wore away at Nick's ability to think. He hated the way she got everyone so charged up. And he was tired. He probably should have stayed home, after all.

But if he left now, he would draw attention. Even an act as simple as obeying the call of nature might be interpreted as a sign of poor commitment to the Movement. Someone might follow him, suspecting him of being a Hardinian, and alert the police.

On the other hand, being cowardly was not the right way to live. Especially in a free country.

He closed his eyes and concentrated. He visualized himself standing on a grand stage, pulling Abbot the Rabbit out of a deep black hat and everyone applauding wildly. Feeling confident and in control, Nick opened his eyes and quickly got up, ignoring the stunned stares from those around him.

He walked across the lush green parliament lawn, feeling a light breeze caressing the back of his neck. Chuckling to himself over his pseudo "Great Disappearing Act," he decided he wouldn't glance over his shoulder. About a hundred feet from the outskirts of the crowd, he turned toward Wellington Street to make his way home, looking forward to getting some much-needed sleep.

Nick slowed. A few paces ahead, a group of mankeys stood in a semicircle, staring down at a large flag of the World Federation spread out on the grass. Their pants were halfway down to their knees. They were urinating on the overlapping orange and black circles at the flag's centre.

A police officer spotted them. Moving quickly, she approached the mankeys and shouted at them that what they were doing was illegal and unhygienic, as the urine could easily spill onto the grass where people needed to walk. One of the mankeys raised his chin and said something about a protest permit, while his neighbour, still urinating, bent forward, reached into his pocket and produced a slip of paper, which he handed to the officer. She smoothed it out and studied it, nodding a few times.

"Okay. Next time try not to block traffic," she finally said, returning the slip of paper to the mankey.

Nick glanced around. A few passersby were eyeing the drenched flag while shaking their heads, pained expressions on their faces.

Nick shrugged. *The price to pay for our freedoms.* He resumed walking.

A minute later, as Nick neared Wellington Street, loud bangs in quick succession jolted his nerves. *Gunshots?*

He gulped air. Women and mankeys ran in every direction, screaming. Nick watched in horror.

To his left, a dozen people in balaclavas locked arms and chanted, "Bring back the family" and "Restore the natural order." Others wielded placards with photos of children and families.

Aerosol clouds formed about fifty feet away.

Nick's eyes watered and stung. People were coughing. He gagged and choked as phlegm filled his lungs.

Up ahead, a line of motorcycle cops gathered, so close they bumped wheels. Holding their batons high, the helmeted women pounded their riot shields.

A helicopter, appearing out of nowhere, hovered over the crowd. The noise was deafening before the aircraft slowly receded.

"She's been shot," a voice rang out.

Heads turned. It was a woman in a wheelchair. Her caregiver grabbed hold of the woman as her head slumped to one side.

"Who shot her? Who would do this?" the caregiver shrieked, looking around frantically.

Nick wanted to run, but his slippered feet wouldn't move, as if glued to the spot.

After catching his breath, he hastened toward the street, away from the chaos, the madness, but his legs were shaking, and twice he stumbled and nearly fell.

Soon he found himself in the direct path of a group of marching men holding a white bedsheet between them, with thick red letters painted on it.

A slender man with cropped hair in a tight T-shirt, blue jeans and black sneakers, marched in front of the banner, blocking some of the words from Nick's view. "...HEAD OF EVERY MAN IS CHRIST. THE HEAD OF EVERY WOMAN IS HER HUSBAND—1 CORINTHIANS 11:3."

The man shouted something incoherent. His face was tense and his eyes full of fire.

His gaze fell on Nick.

Nick swallowed and tried to look away.

"Hey, guy! Are you a man or a mankey?"

Nick's heart beat wildly.

The man halted and his followers stopped in unison. "Are you content with being half a man?" He yelled every word.

Nick said nothing. He didn't understand the question and was afraid of getting drawn into a militant ideology.

"Come, join us, brother! Burn those slippers! For God's sake—for humanity's sake—join the Hardinians before it's too late!" The man extended an open hand.

Nick froze, unsure what to do. The world blurred and voices didn't make sense. Perspiration from his armpits trickled down his trunk, and he trembled.

Severed Roots

Please God, don't let my knees give out. He turned to the side and skirted the group, pretending he was in a hurry to get somewhere.

After walking a full block east along Wellington, Nick stopped and took a few deep breaths. He rubbed his eyes and nose, then glanced at his shaking hands. He'd never been this rattled.

He realized where he needed to go. He turned right and headed straight for Beatrice's house.

CHAPTER EIGHT

Beatrice ambled through Amazon Mall's drugstore, casually surveying the shelves. A small packet caught her eye: antidiarrhea caplets. *Hmm...* In recent weeks she had been running to the bathroom more frequently than usual. She attributed it to stress—her birthday was approaching.

A soothing voice interrupted the soft background music. "Attention, valued shoppers. In honour of Age of Oppression Memorial Day, our orange-and-black memorial candles are half price. Also, be sure to check out the colour portraits of the Advisor in aisle six."

Beatrice cringed at the mention of the Advisor. Pivoting away from the shelf, she brushed against a young woman in a bright orange dress and gasped, staring at her protruding belly.

The woman turned to her. "Is something wrong?"

Beatrice lowered her gaze to a cracked cream-coloured floor tile next to the woman's sandals. "Uh, no—I'm fine." She looked up and forced a smile.

Severed Roots

The pregnant woman raised her eyebrows.

"I mean," Beatrice stammered, "it's not every day one encounters a human manufacturer."

"Not too many of us around," the woman said.

"Is it, uh, interesting work?"

"Interesting?" She looked pensive. "A good thing about the job is that only sperm is involved. A mankey doesn't have to touch me."

Beatrice wrinkled her nose.

"Although, to tell you the truth," the woman continued, leaning in and lowering her voice to a near-whisper, "I often think there's something perverse about it. I mean, I know it sounds crazy and selfish, but there are moments I want to keep the baby...for myself." She dropped her gaze.

Moments? Just moments? Beatrice knew she could never get such a job herself. She was almost thirty. In her younger years, the government had come up with all kinds of excuses to reject her applications, even though the demand for surrogates was high. Although they never said so, it was obvious they considered her unreliable, a flight risk.

"Are you carrying a girl or—"

"A little mankey." She patted her tummy. "Just to meet the quota, of course. My first four were girls."

"Was it hard to get the job?"

The woman examined her up and down. After a moment, she replied in measured tones, "I was never keen on a nine-to-five routine. So I applied for this. The selection process is quite rigorous. They assess you physically and psychologically." The woman sucked in a quick breath and released it. "Y'know, there aren't too many public service jobs like mine, so in a way, I consider myself lucky."

"Yes, you *are* lucky," Beatrice said, though deep down she wasn't sure the job made it worth saying goodbye to your own babies forever.

"Thanks," the woman said. "And..."

"Yes?"

The woman shrugged. "Uh, forget what I said earlier about sometimes wanting to keep the baby. Damn hormones. They mess with your mind."

Beatrice flashed a cold smile and walked away. She chewed on her lower lip as she joined the line at the counter marked "Ministry Issued Prescriptions."

When she returned home, Beatrice removed a small paper bag from her purse and hurried to the bathroom. She tore open the bag in a single motion, twisted the lid off the prescription container inside and poured the contents into the toilet.

"There," she declared, anchoring her hands on her hips. "You can lead this feral horse to water, but you can't make her drink." She stared at the dozens of oblong orange capsules a little longer than usual before flushing.

Nick rang the bell and waited in front of Beatrice's door, shifting from one foot to the other. His legs were still shaking after his terrifying experience on Parliament Hill, but his heart rate had returned to normal.

"Who's there?" asked Beatrice, her voice quavering.

"Nick Wong."

The door swung open.

"Nick! Hey, what's the matter? You look agitated." Beatrice pulled him inside.

She was dressed casually, as always. The sight of her loose pink top and faded blue jeans helped soothe his frayed nerves.

"Have a seat. I'll get you a drink."

Nick lowered himself onto the squeaky couch and tried to relax. He shut his eyes, then changed his mind and reopened them, trying to focus. Everything in Beatrice's living room was from another time. Her place had the feel and smell of an arts centre. Her three-legged wooden chair with the rope seat and her plywood lounge chair were oddly matched with a brown, laminated oval table.

Beatrice's fascination with pottery-making seemed to have grown in the months since his last visit. Her electric potter's wheel supported a partially shaped piece of clay alongside a dirty potter's knife. She was talented, and her many earthenware figures of people and animals sat on shelves and on the windowsills.

Nick's eyes fell on her latest: sculptures of mankeys holding hands with children and mankeys cradling infants. He winced and readjusted his weight on the sofa.

Beatrice appeared with a glass of water and a plate of sliced cheese and carrot sticks. She set both on the coffee table and sat beside him.

"You've been busy," Nick said.

"It's my outlet." She looked out the window.

Nick drank half the cool water.

She turned back toward him. "So, what's going on?"

Nick reached for a couple of cheese slices. "Parliament Hill is a war zone." Between nibbles, he told her the whole story, from the Advisor's ranting on the large screen to the gunshots and tear gas. "I was wandering the streets in a daze. Then I remembered you lived nearby. I knew you'd be off work because of Memorial Day."

She brought her hands to her chest. "Thank goodness you weren't hurt."

Nick leaned forward, steepled his hands and pressed the fingertips to his lips. "What a mad world!"

Beatrice gently pulled Nick's hands away from his face, held them and peered into his eyes. "I'm glad you came, Nick."

Nick nodded. He looked past her at a figure of a man in a top hat and moustache sitting beside a woman on a bench, a baby carrier between them. The man's fingers curled in a protective grip around the handle of the carrier, while his sculpted eyes looked calmly and steadily into the distance, as if to an assured future.

What's behind those peaceful chiselled eyes? What is the man thinking? What does he dream of?

Nick continued gazing at the sculpture, then shook himself out of his reverie. "I guess you're glad to have the day off." It came out as a statement—and a stupid one at that.

Beatrice sighed. "Every day I drag myself to the lab. Adjust knobs. Generate graphs. Produce reports. My day is one big, fat yawn."

Nick squirmed in his seat. *Why is she still holding my hands?* He pulled them away and made a sweeping gesture across the room. "I guess you'd be happier if you could do *this* all day."

Beatrice followed Nick's gesture and straightened her back. "I love the feel of clay between my fingers. I love rolling it into a ball, flattening it, squeezing it, shaping it, smelling it. But I could never make a living from it."

Not surprising. Who would buy your latest sculptures? "It must be lonely work," said Nick.

"I don't mind working alone." Beatrice turned her gaze away. "At the lab, during breaks, people talk a lot but say nothing. Everyone's afraid to talk about what they feel deep down."

"Why?"

"I guess they wouldn't know how to handle it. So they cover up their pain with meaningless chatter."

"And you?"

"I keep quiet. I wait for the day to end so I can come home and restore my sanity."

Hmm. Restore your sanity by creating scandalous artwork.

Nick got up, stepped across the rug and reached for the figurine of a woman holding a baby. He returned to his seat and slowly rotated the pottery in his hands.

He eyed Beatrice. "Still discarding your medication?"

Beatrice nodded. "All day I walk around feeling… empty-handed. Like I should be cradling something in my arms. I know if I took the pills, the feeling would go away, but—I can't explain it—I'd rather feel empty-handed than not feel anything at all."

Nick swallowed. Did Beatrice still plan to set herself on fire? He was afraid raising the question might rekindle her determination to do so. On the other hand, how could he apologize for his callous behaviour toward her a few days ago in the mall if he never brought it up? But maybe today wasn't the day to apologize. He needed to consider carefully what he wanted to say, and he was too unsettled to think clearly.

"In fact," Beatrice continued, "when I heard the doorbell, I panicked. I was afraid it was a surprise visit from the mental health department to test my blood and find out whether I've been taking my meds. I sometimes imagine them locking me up in a psych ward." Her voice quivered.

The mental health department—that's where Karla's new job is. Nick tried to imagine Karla locking up his best friend, and shuddered. A jolt of pain shot through his right temple, and he rubbed his scalp. Was he getting a migraine? He didn't want it to happen in Beatrice's presence, saddling her with more of his problems. He stood. "I need to go."

"So soon?" Beatrice frowned. "But you just got here. You're safer inside."

Nick glanced around. "Yeah...like a turtle." Heat flushed through his body as he contemplated his words.

Beatrice stared at Nick.

"We're turtles. All of us"—he raised his voice—"withdrawing into our shells while the world runs amok."

Beatrice stood and faced him. "Nick, I love hearing you talk this way!" Her eyes were wide and glowing.

Nick's heartbeat strengthened. "It's just that... people don't *question* things. No one seems interested in knowing what's true and what's false. They just stick to whichever side of the fence they happen to be on."

Beatrice smiled. "You're a truth seeker, Nick, aren't you? I've always liked that side of you."

"I-I just wish...I could tell the difference between what is true and real and what is illusion."

"You will," said Beatrice, squeezing Nick's forearm. "It may take time, but you will. I know it."

Beatrice walked Nick to the door.

Nick swiveled to face her. "Speaking of illusion, I'm doing a big show at Goldilocks on the twenty-fourth. Hope you can come."

Beatrice's smile extended from ear to ear. "I wouldn't miss it for the world."

Severed Roots

As Nick walked toward the intersection, a loud siren sounded. He looked around. Motorists, cyclists, and pedestrians were stopping.

Taking his cue from the others, Nick put his feet together and bowed his head for the Minute of Silence. He gazed at his pink slippers while reflecting on the victims of male violence across the millennia.

A piercing note signaled the end of the minute, and the flow of traffic resumed. Nick started walking. He stopped. A thought occurred to him: *Today most of the world is free of male violence and oppression, so why is no one celebrating that?* Nick brought his feet together again, lifted his right hand toward his face, and gazed at the tattoo. He reflected on Beatrice's words when she'd announced her plan to self-immolate: "I no longer want to live in a world like this."

Maybe it was time Nick really tried to understand the world his best friend was referring to.

CHAPTER NINE

Nick pulled out his handkerchief and wiped the sweat from his forehead. The air was humid, and rows of bright-yellow daffodils lit up the front lawns.

It was one o'clock on Friday afternoon, the usual time for Morrie's lesson. Morrie had been showing up for his lessons, raring to learn, over the past two weeks. But today Nick was performing, and he'd invited Morrie to accompany him.

"I fell into magic when I was about six," he said, as he and Morrie waited for the city bus to Goldilocks Children's Theatre.

"What brings a six-year-old to explore magic?"

They stood by the curb, a large duffel bag slumped between them with the words "Nick McTrick" scrawled on the side in red paint.

"I was at the Children's Centre then. I realized that only the girls, who lived on the upper floor, had birthday parties. For the boys, birthdays were just announced—there would be no cake, no candles, no song. So, I had this crazy idea to make a small birthday celebration for a random kid. It would be a surprise. I would build a box with a hidden compartment. It would contain a miniature birthday cake. The box would appear empty when I first opened it. But after I closed it, I would angle it slightly. When I showed the inside again, everyone would see that the box magically contained a cake. We'd then sing 'Happy Birthday.'"

"A veritable child prodigy," Morrie said, tapping a forefinger against his temple.

Nick was happy having Morrie with him. He felt a warmth when he was talking to him, like that first sip of hot cocoa that enters your stomach. Yes, warmth and comfort all in one. Wiping another stream of perspiration off his neck, he gazed at the tuft of dry chest hairs peeking out from Morrie's open-collared black shirt. Was the man too at ease with the world to sweat?

"I worked it all out in my head, and during arts and crafts, I took small pieces of wood and glued the box together. I used modeling clay to make a cake. When I finished, I felt proud of myself. I showed the facilitator my magic trick. She smiled and said nothing. The next day, she took me aside and said, 'Magic is like lying.' She made me throw out the box. I cried for days."

Morrie's eyes went wide. "Horrific and despicable!"

Nego Huzcotoq

The city bus pulled up. Its side panel displayed an old woman awkwardly occupying a park swing, and a line of young people queuing behind, arms folded across their chests. Above the old woman the caption read: YOU HAD YOUR FUN. DON'T BE A BURDEN. VISIT DYINGWITHDIGNITY.COM.

The doors opened and they got on. "Fortunately, my next facilitator had the wisdom to consult with the Netbot and discovered magic wasn't really lying. It was entertainment. I was allowed to continue my hobby, and two months later we celebrated Friedrich's fifth birthday."

"Thank God for that." Morrie hastened to pay the bus fares for both of them.

"Thanks, Morrie," Nick said. "There was no need to do that." *And thank you, Angelina*, Nick whispered to himself. *Thank you for allowing me to continue my magic.*

Goldilocks Children's Theatre had a wide stage with a sunken orchestra pit in the front. A hundred and fifty little girls and their facilitators filled the theatre. There were no boys. Boys were taken on outings separately and less often.

Nick hadn't performed for kids in months. Ever since he'd graduated from the Children's Centre at the age of sixteen, he'd felt increasingly uneasy around them. He wasn't sure why—maybe because they reminded him of his own lonesome childhood. When he did do shows for children, he always had to force himself to push through the setup and the first few minutes of performance. Then the magic took over.

Today, Nick had an additional reason to feel on edge: Morrie. Nick's sleights of hand had to be executed flawlessly for his astute student. He fervently hoped he wouldn't get a migraine attack during his show, as sometimes happened when he was under prolonged stress.

The audience sat mesmerized as Nick McTrick spun his magic. On stage, a skinny girl who'd been called up threw her head back with widening eyes as he made red balls disappear and reappear in her hands. Working the audience, Nick reached behind a flabby-faced girl's ear and pulled out a mysterious purple light. The rosy-cheeked facilitator, sitting next to her in the front row, gasped when the purple light turned into a bellflower as he handed it to the girl. Yellow silk scarves rose and fell gracefully in the air, without visible support, and when Nick linked solid steel rings, applause erupted.

Nick spotted Beatrice in the back row, laughing.

After the show, she ran up to the stage. "You always transform yourself into a totally different person while you're performing."

Nick shrugged. "It's the top hat and wand."

"I think it's the children. You become funny and outrageous. That's the *real* magic."

Nick rocked on his heels.

Morrie, who Nick had insisted sit in the front row as his special guest, appeared next to him, with a cry of "Bravo, my boy!" and a friendly slap on the back.

Nick introduced Morrie to Beatrice.

"Come often?" Morrie asked.

Beatrice pushed her blond hair off the side of her face. "I love magic. It's an escape from our everyday lives."

"Pity we need to escape from our lives. What do you do?"

"For a woman, I'm a bit of an oddity—a simple lab assistant."

As Morrie and Beatrice continued chatting, Nick led them backstage. Beatrice and Morrie sat on a dusty sofa, using the half that wasn't occupied by old sound equipment. Nick grabbed a rickety wooden chair from nearby and plopped down on it, letting his black magician's cape fall gracefully over the chair's back. For a fleeting moment he feared the seat would collapse under his weight, but he feigned nonchalance, giving his friends his best casual smile.

"Ever consider becoming a magician yourself?" Morrie asked Beatrice.

"No," she said. "You need quick hands. I move like a sloth."

"Are you good at keeping secrets?"

"Yes—no—actually, I can't tell you." She smiled, and Morrie and Nick laughed. "I do wonder, though, why magicians are still mostly men."

"Some things never change," said Morrie. "Men like to show off. They like having secret knowledge."

Nick squirmed in his chair.

Morrie winked at Nick. "Not our Nick, mind you. He's just talent, pure and simple."

Morrie threw that in to be nice. Was Morrie right, though, about a need to show off? Why would Morrie want magic lessons then? He seemed the opposite of insecure.

"As for women," Morrie continued, "they're magical in and of themselves. They never needed gimmicks. The ability to conjure up life from seemingly nothing—albeit in nine months—is the greatest magic of all."

"I guess today you'd have to call that black magic," Beatrice said flatly, crossing her arms and sinking deeper into the sofa. Her chin jutted out.

Nick chuckled nervously. He wobbled the chair underneath to reassure himself it was still stable enough. He looked at Morrie, who wore a crooked smile.

"Yes, the dark art..." Morrie twisted sideways so he could face Beatrice. He raised his hands to eye level and moved his fingers like a crawling spider. Using a creepy accent, he proclaimed, "If you even attempt to have a baby, you'll be thrown into a dungeon. Later, you'll be stripped, blindfolded, gagged, tied to a pole on top of a pyre...and *burned*."

Nick's mouth fell open. How could Morrie have said that to Beatrice, even if only playfully?

"I suppose it is...something like that." Beatrice hung her head.

Nick forced himself to look at her. Her eyes shone with unshed tears. In that instant, he understood why she'd come that afternoon. Because it was a children's show, and she was happy being around children. She delighted in hearing their laughter and feeling their excitement.

Nick had to admit that he had enjoyed seeing the girls' faces during his show. With a successful performance behind him, he felt bold in his cape, high-collared white shirt, and dark-purple bow tie. And now was the perfect opportunity to gauge whether his best friend was serious about suicide. He glanced around and took a deep breath. "Beatrice, what do you think? I mean, if one can't have children...is life still worth living?"

Beatrice sat unmoving, her gaze frozen on Nick. She seemed unable to speak.

In a flash, her face puffed up and her eyes reddened.

Severed Roots

"Can you miss something you never had?" She choked on her words. "Can you desire what society says you shouldn't?" She turned to Morrie. Her chin trembled. "I was di-diagnosed with motherhood syndrome."

Morrie nodded, keeping a neutral expression.

Beatrice paused, and her eyes welled. "All I want is a little boy or girl to hold and care for. Is that so bad? Women say they have no use for children, but"—her voice sounded cracked and strained—"was there ever a mother in history who didn't love her baby?" Tears rolled down her cheeks.

Nick looked down and thought of Angelina, how distraught she'd been when she gave up her son to the Children's Centre. He eyed the black-and-white wand that lay by his feet. If only he could pick it up, wave it and make Beatrice's tears stop!

Shifting in his seat, he raised his eyebrows at Morrie. Morrie gave a tiny nod and put a hand on Beatrice's shoulder, waiting until she stopped crying. Then, he whispered something in her ear, and a slight smile formed on her face. Morrie ignored Nick's inquisitive look and stood, indicating it was time to leave.

As Nick got up, he fumbled for words, but stopped when Morrie brought a forefinger to his lips.

Nick changed and the three of them left the backstage area. After Beatrice reassured Nick and Morrie that she was okay, they said their goodbyes.

As Beatrice ambled toward the washroom, Nick fervently hoped that she was really okay and wouldn't do anything rash.

Morrie turned to Nick as they reached the exit. "Tell me, Nick. Do you believe people like Beatrice are mentally ill?"

Nick pulled in a deep breath and slowly released it. "Either they are or society is."

Morrie smiled as they stepped into the warm afternoon drizzle. "Come to my place for dinner next Thursday, and we'll talk more." As Morrie headed in a different direction to his bus stop, he waved over his shoulder. "Thanks for today. I enjoyed it."

A warmth radiated through Nick's chest. *I've made a friend, a real friend.*

CHAPTER TEN

The next morning, Nick's head throbbed; it felt like an axe had been wedged into his brain. He opened his eyes, and his stomach contracted violently. As he struggled to pull himself up from his floor mattress, chunks of last night's Kraft dinner splattered onto the mattress and hardwood floor. *Damn.* His vision blurred. Bolts of pain shot through his temples, and he clutched his head, groaning. *This is the worst ever.* He wiped his mouth with the edge of his T-shirt while a sour stench filled his nostrils. He staggered to his phone, trying to avoid the mess, and called for an ambulance.

His world turned black.

When his eyes flickered open, someone was leaning over him. The person slowly came into focus, a petite woman with grave brown eyes and a pinched mouth. She wore a white lab coat and smelled of disinfectant. The woman coldly informed him he was on the second floor of Grace Hospital, in the neurology unit, and had been there since he was admitted five hours earlier.

"MRI angiography, lumbar puncture, and neuroimaging results indicate an unusual and acute form of neurovascular inflammation," she said, her face stern. "We have not yet been able to identify the cause."

Nick had difficulty following but didn't want to risk annoying her by asking for clarification.

"We'll keep you here for further tests until we can determine the best course of action. In the meantime, you'll need to fill this out."

She helped him into a sitting position, handed him a form and left.

Nick looked around. An IV pole and a heart monitor stood against the white wall in front, along with other large equipment with knobs and displays. At the foot of his bed, a small table on wheels held gauze, gloves, and other supplies.

A cold, sterile place.

He completed the form mechanically. One question asked if there was anyone he wished to have notified. He left it blank.

Over the next twenty hours, the doctors subjected Nick to a battery of tests. They scanned, poked, prodded and squeezed, hardly ever looking him in the eye. Thankfully, the sharp, searing pain in his head subsided, leaving a dull ache.

Severed Roots

His mind drifted to Angelina, and he tried to imagine the endless tests and procedures she'd likely endured. Was she still living at home? Or had they moved her to Franklin House? Wait—Angelina had said Franklin House was part of Grace Hospital.

Maybe he should call her. Be proactive for once. He couldn't recall a single time he'd phoned or visited her that wasn't because of her request.

What would it be like, having a real, healthy connection with her? Maybe it was time he tried it.

Nothing to lose.

He reached over the bedrails for the phone on his bedside table and keyed in her home number, fearing the number might be forwarded to Franklin House.

She answered on the fourth ring. "Hello?"

Nick swallowed, feeling light-headed.

"Hello?" Angelina repeated, a nervous edge to her voice.

"Uh, hi, Angelina. How are you?"

"Nick? I was going to call you. I was admitted to Franklin two days ago."

Nick strained to hear her voice over the hum of the air exchanger.

"Nico..." A string of harsh coughs hammered his ear. "It's unbearable." More coughing. "Call me later."

Nick sighed as he tapped off the phone. Just then, the curtain was pulled back and an attendant appeared with his lunch. Nick was able to learn from him that Franklin House was two floors up, in the same wing.

I could see Angelina in a few minutes. She'd be surprised and happy.

Nick decided to wait until he'd eaten to drop in on her.

The meal was a plate of soggy pasta and metallic-tasting peas. A bottle of tomato juice stood in the place of the can of Coke he'd naively envisioned accompanying the meal. There was no dessert. *Oh well, at least the meal was hot,* he consoled himself as he transferred the last bits of food onto his plastic fork.

After adjusting his hospital gown, he hobbled over to the elevator, glad the nurses hadn't hooked him to the IV pole. As he reached for the button, he shuddered, recalling from his last visit at her home the poor wasted woman she'd become. He hesitated. Did he really want to see her in so much pain?

He returned to his room, paced up and down a few times and then called her again. Not knowing how else to start the conversation, he asked her if she was happy at Franklin House.

"Happy? What do you think? I'm dying!" She sounded shocked and bitter.

"Of course...I meant, besides that." Nick's face and neck turned impossibly hot.

"There is no *besides that!*"

Nick closed his eyes and scolded himself for his stupidity. "I mean...are you being looked after well?"

"The nurses are stressed, rushed. I feel like I'm wasting their time."

No kidding. Not enough caregivers. And the problem will only get worse. Nick had heard that the government's latest proposal to increase the quota of births per surrogate from nine to twelve was rejected by the Human Manufacturers Union. "What about the pain?"

"It's constant. Every single moment...even when I'm asleep."

"Uh...don't the medications help?"

A long pause. "For the pain, somewhat, but there is no medication for loneliness."

Nick didn't know what else to say. Maybe he should have visited her earlier, but now it was too late. If he visited her now, she'd figure out from his hospital gown that he was a patient in the same building. She'd be miffed that he had phoned—twice—when he could easily have gone to see her.

Nick wished for a way to end the conversation gracefully. There was a long, awkward silence.

"Nick?" Angelina's voice sounded weak and strained, as if a different woman were talking.

"What's wrong?"

"Nick—Nico, the medical staff here are okay, but I need someone to listen to me with their heart, not just with their ears. I need someone who is interested not only in the progression of the disease and how it's affecting my body. I need someone who will hold me to make me feel better, not because that's their job but because they care about me."

He tightened his grip on the phone and stared at the ceiling. *She's trying to make me feel guilty.*

"Nico...? Nico, I'm—I don't want to die like I lived. I want to die with serenity. I'm ready to meet my Maker and beg for His mercy."

Nick frowned.

"I want to go with a clean slate. Nick, please forgive me for being harsh with you over the years."

Harsh with you over the years? Nick was unsure what to make of that statement. Soon, tears welled behind his eyelids. His thoughts were jumbled, and he had a sudden desire to be cuddled.

"There's nothing to forgive. You've always cared for me like...like a..."

"Mother?"

Nick's throat constricted. "I'll visit you soon." He hung up.

Nick's legs dangled over the cold metal bed rails as he sat, half listening to codes blaring through the intercom and the occasional *ping* of an elevator. The faint smell of bleach emanated from his bedding, bringing a sick taste in his mouth.

Severed Roots

A strange, awful feeling seized him, putting pressure on his chest, preventing him from filling his lungs completely. He realized he had never had frank and intimate conversations with Angelina. She'd always made time for him, but he'd never made enough for her. The missed opportunities, his inability to say "I love you"—even once—now tore at his heart.

Did he love her?

He fell back on the hospital bed and closed his eyes. As he lay on the stiff white mattress in the brightly lit room, thoughts and long-forgotten images of his early years in the Children's Centre drifted into his mind.

Long hallways leading to cavernous rooms. Pungent smells. A sense of being lost and alone. Being afraid to sleep because he might wet his bed. Not wanting to wake up because everyone had to line up at six-thirty but breakfast wasn't served until nine. And when it came, it was more often than not lumpy, half-burned porridge.

"I wan-my-mother!" Nico would scream until his throat hurt. He had no recollection of his mother. The words were just a mantra he'd heard the older boys cry out whenever they were distraught. Some of them remembered their mothers, because they had been older than Nick when the government seized them.

"I wan-my-mother!"

"I wan-my-mother!"

A gentle smile from the facilitator. "Why would you want a mother? Or any parent, for that matter? Parents are selfish and controlling. They had you because they wanted someone they could own. Did your mother or father ever say, 'I love you?' That was *ma-ni-pu-la-tive*."

The memories became more cohesive. Some of the older girls—the seniors—helped teach the younger children. One senior with big, sad eyes was called Miss Laura. She'd once taken Nick aside when he was particularly distraught and said, "You feel like an empty shell day after day, don't you? Like you're nobody and belong nowhere. I cry along with you, Nico. But things will get better soon." Then, softly, she sang the song everyone sang before breakfast.

A world where everything is black or brown or grey
Where birds do not sing, and children do not play,
Where the only sounds are grunts or the cries of battle,
A world where men are masters and women are cattle.

She put her arm around him and continued.

A new world is upon us
Where women are strong and mankeys gentle,

Severed Roots

Where we pursue our mission to transcend our natures
And realize our God-given potential.

Nick cherished the memory of the song, even though he didn't understand its meaning at the time, and he especially cherished Miss Laura's embrace. It had been special, and it had also been one of the rare indications he mattered to someone bigger than himself.

Miss Laura hadn't stayed around long. The seniors graduated and moved on. Nick's facilitators had frequently changed, too, and the boys' sections were continually reshuffled like a deck of cards.

Not so with the girls. They grew up with the same cohort, and their facilitators seldom changed.

The girls occupied the entire upper floor. They were taught science, management, leadership, and other subjects appropriate for girls. At night, and even during the day, the boys often caught snippets of laughter filtering through the ceiling. Oh, how they'd wished they, too, were girls.

As much as the boys had felt abandoned when their facilitators were reassigned, they experienced new depths of loneliness when they were left with only the Netbot.

The Netbot. That shiny mechanical cylinder, gliding along—left, right, forward, back—spinning around itself and stretching its robotic arms outward, holding the touch screen in front of the boys. Inviting interaction.

"Nico, you look sad," it said one day as it rolled up in front of him.

"Alex and Sylvio won't let me play jump rope with them," he'd responded.

"I'll bet that hurt your feelings, Nico."

"Yeah, it made me mad."

"I can see that."

"Why won't they let me play?"

The robot whirred. "Did you talk to them about it?"

"I don't want to."

"Why don't you want to?"

"I don't know."

"Why don't you know? You may want to think about it, and we can talk some more."

The good thing about the Netbot was that it was always available and stayed the same. Still—Nick didn't know why—when he felt angry, sad, lonely or afraid, its queries seemed distant, never comforting.

The Netbot taught them, tested them, asked them questions, gave them assignments. They were told all the facilitators would eventually be replaced with Netbots, since they were infinitely more knowledgeable, analytical, patient and fair.

Severed Roots

Then one day Angelina entered his life. He must have been around eight. She strode into the dormitory while the boys were getting dressed—a slender woman in tinted glasses and with the darkest, thickest curls he had ever seen—and announced she was their new facilitator. Immediately, she started snapping at everyone to hurry to roll call. She behaved like an army sergeant, and everyone feared her. But over the months, she mellowed. During that time, Nick was increasingly whiny around her, always seeking her attention.

Nick had felt detached from the other boys and carers—except Angelina. He often kept to himself, but at times he bullied the smaller kids. When that happened, Angelina would sometimes pour a teaspoon of "calming juice" into his drink or soup, but more often she would just reprimand him. She seemed to care about his behaviour even if he didn't care much about it himself.

Nick emerged from the past and opened his eyes. He remembered with clarity how Angelina had used the forbidden word: *mother*.

He tugged at the bedsheet, pulling it loose from its tight corner folds and winced at the hospital smell as he tucked it closer under his chin.

Did she see herself as a kind of mother to him? He didn't know who his real parents were, but did it matter?

Angelina had once spoken to him about her own father, how he would refer to Angelina and her sister as his flock and to himself as their shepherd.

Interestingly, at the time Nick had felt sorry not for her but for himself. Even though he hadn't understood why, he had harboured a deep longing for someone older, someone wiser than himself in his life. A person who would always care for him, protect him and make him feel important.

Was that what parents were for? Maybe they weren't people who just owned and controlled you. There might be more to it.

Nick stared at a fold in the bedsheet below his chin. He curled his hands into tight fists.

Now Angelina was dying. The only person he knew who cared for him as a "mother" was about to die, and in all these years he hadn't really understood their relationship.

"I hate myself. I hate myself," he muttered. "I hate my life. I hate my past. I'll never be content, and I'll die poor, miserable and alone."

Nick threw his hands over his face. His breathing, shallow and rapid, suddenly slowed. He slid his fingers apart slightly and stared at the white wall for a long time.

Maybe he could just...end it.

Yes, that could be the answer. It's got to be quick and painless. I'll steal the strongest medication on this floor and take an overdose.

There's no point in going on.

I hate this meaningless existence. I hate my ape brain, my oversized body and my mouth that always says the wrong things.

Or...

There might be another solution.

The billboard near Amazon Mall he'd seen many times flashed into his mind.

Maybe I should go for the operation. Mankeys who've done it seem happy, proud of themselves for taking their future into their own hands and making something worthwhile of themselves.

But that would mean having his body parts mutilated and reconstructed and taking hormone replacement therapy for the rest of his life. Also, he had not grown up as a girl. His body would be female, but would *he* be?

Or maybe I should do both—the gender switch and then the off switch. I could die as a woman.

Flopping onto his back, Nick lay tangled in the sheets, one arm dangling over the side of the narrow bed. *Is it worth going through such a painful procedure for a taste of dignity? A more respectable funeral?*

No, better to just end it now.

He would observe everything around him. He would interview nurses and talk to other patients. He would find out—trying not to raise suspicion—where the medications were stored and which ones were the most potent.

He set a deadline. By midnight tomorrow he'd be dead.

As Nick was concocting his plan, another thought crept up in his fatigued mind. *Stealing medications is wrong.*

He needed a better solution.

Wait! This was a hospital. So there might be a Dying with Dignity clinic nearby. These days, every major hospital had one. He'd need to correctly answer a simple math question to confirm his cognitive clarity, and—*pronto*—he'd be allowed to end his misery with a supervised lethal injection.

Thank God for our freedoms.

As Nick was mulling this over, a nurse entered. Another test? A waste of time.

Nick sat up, smirking—he had a secret goal. "How are you?" he said.

The nurse eyed him strangely. "You have a visitor."

"A visitor?"

At that moment, a woman he knew well appeared from behind the curtain with a friendly smile and a bouquet of daisies.

CHAPTER ELEVEN

Karla sported the navy blue business suit she always wore, even when she was off work.

Nick had never seen her look so tired. Her eyes drooped, showing fine wrinkles at the corners. She sat on the edge of his bed. "You didn't return my messages. I figured something must be wrong, so I called the nearest hospital."

A towering male nurse stepped into the room with snacks. Karla stood and demanded to see Nick's medical charts. She inquired about his diagnosis and treatment plan, the side effects of the prescribed medications, his recommended diet and activities during his hospital stay. The nurse stammered incoherent bits of information and backed into the corridor. Karla turned to Nick and asked how he felt, if the food was adequate and whether he needed anything at all.

It was good having Karla there, though he wished he knew why she cared about him so much.

"You'd better get well fast 'cause I've a great job for you," Karla said while Nick played with his canned fruit salad. "Listen, I can't stay long." She looked away.

Nick's spoon hovered midway to his mouth. "What's wrong?"

"I guess you haven't been following the news."

Nick's stomach churned.

"There's renewed fear of an uprising. Here and in the US."

Nick put down his spoon. "Can't anything be done to prevent it?"

Karla shook her head. "Elections are in three weeks. If the Advisor loses, the Hardinians may take a wait-and-see approach. But that's academic. Latest polls indicate her approval rating is high across the World Federation."

Nick studied Karla's face as she twiddled with the strap of her handbag.

"Nick, the Hardinians issued an ultimatum. We have three months to legalize motherhood, or we brace ourselves for civil war."

Something fluttered in Nick's belly. The prospect of civil war terrified him.

He took a deep breath. "What if the government were to give in to their demand? We'd avoid a blood bath. It takes—what?—nine months to have a baby? Assuming anyone would even want to. So we buy time and…I mean, we figure out something—" Nick had no idea where he was going with this and felt stupid.

"No!" Irritation flashed across Karla's face. "We will never turn back the clock."

Nick narrowed his eyes. *Beatrice has a biological clock, which may be ticking toward doomsday.* "I've a friend who—"

"Beatrice? She has a distorted perspective," Karla snapped. "She lives in the past."

"So why did people in the past want children?" Nick folded his arms in front of his chest.

"You know as well as I do—to show off their possessions. Or to help on the farm. Or so there'd be someone to care for them in their old age. All pure selfishness."

Nick tried to imagine Beatrice as selfish and drew a blank.

As if sensing his thoughts, Karla softened her expression. She sat back down on Nick's bed.

"Nick, I'm sure Beatrice is a decent person. Her body can't help feeling what it feels. I hope her meds will help her get better."

Nick hoped nothing he said or did would betray the fact that Beatrice was discarding her medications.

"You know," Karla continued. "You could help her. Suggest she get a pet."

"A pet? She wants children—and a husband."

"A mankey too? Oh yeah, I remember—from the meeting. Her condition's pretty bad."

"Beatrice doesn't think so." Nick wasn't sure if Beatrice was ill or not, but he felt a need to defend his best friend. Besides, challenging Karla's perspective might help him understand it better.

Karla drew a few slow breaths while smoothing out a corner of the bedsheet.

"Nick. For heavensake. Think. Reflect. Women always wanted men but at the same time lived in mortal fear of them. You learned history, didn't you? In the countryside, women were afraid of traveling at night. In the towns and cities too." Her voice was tired but forceful.

"We installed door locks and gates. We created security systems. Video monitors. Police protection and jails. And even then, women had to hide daggers and spray guns and constantly look over their shoulders. Is that a healthy way to live, Nick? It's pathetic. Oh, to be able to travel freely and enjoy God's beautiful world. To go camping solo and no longer have a greater fear of men than of bears or snakes."

Nick pushed aside the food tray. Of course, he had learned all this. It was drilled into every little mankey in the Children's Centre through story, song and play. Any six-year-old knows that in the Age of Oppression over 95 percent of violent criminals were men.

Severed Roots

Nick shifted his upper body on the inclined bed and stretched his legs, careful not to accidentally brush Karla. He tried to visualize walking along narrow cobblestone streets in a bygone era and woman after woman recoiling from him in fear.

Karla rubbed her forehead and locked eyes with Nick. "Wake up." She spoke softly, nearly whispering. "Look around, Nick. Open your eyes. A new World Order has emerged. We can *almost* walk freely. We can *almost* breathe fresh air. We can *almost* blossom into our full potential. All that threatens us is the holdouts, those intransigent men and women who are trying to bring back the past, the *Hardinians*." Karla spat out the word.

She didn't wait for Nick to respond. Opening her handbag, she removed a rectangular package wrapped in ocean-blue paper.

"A present. I'll drop by tomorrow to see how you're doing." She glanced at the door, gave Nick a quick hug and left.

The memory of Karla's arms around Nick's body lingered even after she'd left, leaving him warm and relaxed. *Hugs have magic power.* Over the years, Karla had hugged Nick a handful of times, usually after darting her eyes from side to side to make sure no one was looking.

He tore open the wrapping. The gift was an elegant maple-coloured mug with a golden handle and a personalized inscription: AN OUNCE OF FRIENDSHIP IS WORTH MORE THAN A POUND OF BLOOD. And underneath, in smaller letters: I WILL ALWAYS BE YOUR FRIEND –KARLA ROOK.

Nick stared at the inscription for a long time. His lips curved up. He couldn't believe that less than a half hour earlier, he'd planned to end his life and now he looked forward to getting out of the hospital and starting his new job with Karla—whatever that would be.

Karla stepped into the hospital elevator and pressed number four. Then she quickly pressed number three and got off on the third floor. She needed a few moments to herself. Finding a quiet spot in a narrow hallway across from the ultrasound room, she slumped onto the floor and leaned her back against the wall.

Does Nick have a right to know? Karla wondered for the thousandth time.

"Nick, I've something important to tell you," she imagined herself saying. *"No, actually, it's not important at all."*

"What is it?" Nick would say, lifting his thick eyebrows.

And she would tell him.

Karla stared at the brown-and-white linoleum flooring.

No, it's better if he doesn't know. Our relationship would no longer be free and pure. I'll talk to Angelina again and impress upon her that it's in Nick's best interest not to know.

Karla scrambled to her feet, shook her head as if to dust off any remnants of ambivalence, and took the stairs one floor up to visit her dying aunt.

CHAPTER TWELVE

It was May 30, three days since Nick had been released from the hospital, armed with migraine pills and stern advice to exercise and eat more healthily. He felt upbeat. The air was crisp, and the sun displayed its brilliance. Yesterday, Morrie had phoned Nick to remind him of tonight's dinner. Nick looked forward to getting to know his quirky friend better.

His only regret was not visiting Angelina in the hospital. How was she doing? Was she thinking of him, hoping he'd show up at her bedside? He had told her he'd visit her, so he should keep his word.

Tomorrow, first thing.

He strolled along Rosemary Avenue, following the directions Morrie had given him, and came upon a group of shirtless men in hard hats repairing the road. A heavyset woman in a yellow safety vest and blue tool belt shouted through a loudspeaker. "Get a grip, mankeys. I said use *less* patching mix. Less mix. Now, smooth it out fast."

Severed Roots

Nick averted his eyes and continued strolling beside a long row of three-story stone mansions, each constructed in a different style and surrounded by mature trees and manicured lawns. Morrie's house seemed to be the last one on the cul-de-sac, set even farther back from the street than the others and behind a gate.

He double-checked the address. When he looked up at the house again, it took a while to sink in that his friend lived there. Nick had assumed Morrie, like almost all mankeys he knew, was on social assistance and likely occupying a dingy basement apartment.

The back of his neck tingled as he forced his feet onward. If Morrie had enough money to live in a mansion, why was he interested in associating with Nick?

Nick stepped inside the gate and inhaled the scent of freshly cut grass. He glanced at his watch. With a start, he realized he was five minutes late. He hurried across the lawn and the veranda to the red door with the large iron knocker.

The door swung open before Nick could knock. Morrie, dressed in black pants, a white shirt and a dark green waistcoat, greeted Nick with a slight bow. "Come in, come in, my boy." Morrie took his arm and pulled him through the doorway. As Nick stepped inside, his eyes widened in awe.

The foyer was capped with a burgundy ceiling rising in a high arch. A wide marble staircase spiraled up to the second floor. To his left, elaborate French doors opened into an enormous living room, which Morrie gestured for him to enter.

The place was unlike anything he'd ever seen except in pictures. Antique chairs surrounded triangular and circular coffee tables. A brass grandfather clock posed haughtily against the wall. A grand piano stood proudly at the far end.

As they reached the middle of the giant area rug, Nick slowed his gait. On the left was a doorless entrance to a den. Two bookshelves crammed with worn-looking books lined its far wall. The tomes looked old enough to be from the Age of Oppression. *Hmm.* Were any of them illegal? Obscene? Hate promoting? Karla had once suggested that 90 percent of books from the Age of Oppression were "grossly inappropriate" and ought to be banned. (And to think, she was a strong proponent of freedom of speech!) In front of the bookcases sat a chair and ottoman, and next to them stood a round glass-top coffee table on three curved wooden legs. He zeroed in on the object on top of the glass: a shiny handgun.

Nick's heart raced.

As if sensing Nick's reaction, Morrie flicked his wrist in the direction of the den. "I have enemies. People are jealous of my good looks."

Nick swallowed. *Why so flippant?* When they reached the end of the living room, having walked past the grand piano, Morrie bowed again, ushering Nick through another set of double doors.

Nick inhaled sharply. Dominating the dining room was a long table laid out with decorated china, sparkling wine glasses, red cloth napkins and tall white candles. There were seven chairs and place settings.

Nick's jaw slackened. Nothing had prepared him for such a sight. Who else was invited?

Morrie, positioning himself at the head of the table, gestured for Nick to sit next to him. As he took his seat, Nick glanced at his shabby sweatshirt and faded blue jeans and considered his presence a stain on the opulent surroundings.

A tall, slender woman with vibrant eyes and thin lips appeared from an adjoining door, followed closely by four children. The faces of the children displayed, in different variations, some of the same features as those of the tall woman but were animated with charming, curious frowns.

Nick gripped the side of his chair. *Hardinians! They must keep these children hidden in the cellar. I've fallen in with criminals!*

Morrie's eyes twinkled as he spoke. "Nick, meet my lovely wife, Hanna, and our children—Rebecca, Stephen, Daniel and Nathalie."

Wife? Yet the woman beamed with pride. Nick felt as if he had landed in a topsy-turvy world.

He grimaced. He should report everything to the authorities—the illegal books, the children, Hanna. But then he remembered the gun on the coffee table. *What do they use the gun for?* His leg muscles tensed.

"A pleasure to meet you," Hanna said, with a slight bow and a nervous edge to her voice. Then she excused herself from the room. The children calmly took their seats around the table. They ranged in age from about five to thirteen. The boys wore chocolate-coloured suits and matching striped ties, and the girls were adorned in flowery, knee-length dresses.

Such an odd sight. He'd never seen little mankeys in suits. And the girls! They might as well have dropped in from a previous century.

A torrent of questions flooded Nick's mind. *Why did Morrie choose to reveal his illegal activities? How does he manage to keep his family a secret from the world? How did he become so wealthy?*

He decided it was safest to adopt a casual style of inquiry.

"What do you do with them?" Nick asked, surprising himself with the provocative question. "The children, that is."

Pairs of curious eyes jumped from him to Morrie.

Severed Roots

"What do you mean 'what do I do with them?'" Morrie replied, with a touch of indignation. "I guide them. I listen to them. I talk to them. I play with them. I give them what they need, sometimes what they want."

Nick's thoughts whirled. He worried for the children. Their parents owned and controlled them. He rubbed his hands on his pants legs. *Morrie and Hanna can do whatever they want to those helpless children, and no one would even know.* He fixed his gaze on the draperies across the room, seeking inspiration from their deep-purple colour. "Uh, so you think people should replace the Netbot as the provider of guidance and advice to children?" His mouth turned dry.

"Great question!" Morrie's demeanour relaxed. "My kids actually *prefer* coming to me for advice and guidance, and I expect them to do so. The Netbot has its uses. But it can't share life experiences, impart values, give love."

"What about the Children's Centres?"

"What about them?" Morrie sounded irritated.

"Can you raise children better than the centres do?"

Morrie was silent for a moment. "Tell me something. To whom do you belong?"

Nick frowned, not understanding the question.

"Every person," Morrie said, "belongs—to a group, a team, a movement..."

"I, uh, belong...to the human race."

"The human race!" Morrie smirked. "I'm glad it's not to another part of the animal kingdom. Listen, ask my Nathalie to whom she belongs, and she'll tell you she belongs to this family. Now, if you ask any other member of my family, 'Who belongs to you?' they'll list everyone and include Nathalie. We all know Nathalie—what she likes, what she doesn't like, what makes her laugh, what makes her angry. If I ask members of the human race who belongs to them, will they include *you* in their answer? Do they know you at all? That, my friend, is the difference."

Rebecca, grinning with obvious pride at her father's wisdom, gave orders to her younger siblings to tie their napkins around their necks, then disappeared into the kitchen. Hanna reappeared, carrying a tray with bowls of steaming soup. Rebecca followed closely, her chin high, and distributed the bowls—to her father, then to Nick, and finally to her siblings. With a gleam in her eyes, she carefully placed the last bowl where her mother would be seated.

The scene felt strange. Only on rare occasions—such as at Angelina's—had Nick been served a meal by a female. In the Children's Centre, a boy or young mankey distributed the food. Nick looked at Rebecca, at her silky black hair and charming smile. There was no air of subservience about her. She acted with poise and grace and even seemed to take pride in her serving skills.

Nick began gulping down his soup but paused when he noticed everyone else taking their time eating. Although he wanted to ask more questions, it was fascinating just to watch this odd collection of people sitting together and savouring the minestrone over the crackling sounds from the nearby fireplace. No one spoke, except that Stephen and Daniel occasionally exchanged glances and giggled.

After the soup, Morrie broke out in song, while Hanna and Rebecca again excused themselves from the dining room. Nick had never heard the song before. It was melodic and uplifting and had something to do with the virtues of a mother and of a spouse.

Morrie stood and glided around the dining table. Still singing, he grabbed Daniel's and Nathalie's hands, their little faces gushing pleasure, and danced with them in a circle in front of the deep-purple draperies.

Her value is more than any treasure...

Stomping his feet, kicking them high, swaying his arms and twisting his torso—left, right, toward the floor, toward the ceiling—while Nick looked on in amazement.

Her kindness and goodness beyond measure...

Hanna popped her head in through the kitchen door, her cheeks glowing, and smiled at the spectacle.

Morrie released his children's hands and began jumping to a quickened tempo with such buoyancy it seemed he would take off like a bird at any moment.

He returned to his seat, drenched in sweat. Breathing heavily, he looked Nick straight in the eyes. "Life is good," he said, as if he were revealing the secret of the universe.

Nick stared at Morrie, slack-jawed. "What... where do you get that kind of stamina? Your strength?"

Still panting, Morrie slid off his chair and ambled over to the purple draperies, motioning for Nick to follow.

Morrie pulled the draperies to one side, revealing a towering red oak against a low hanging sun. The bark was scaly and grey, with patches of reddish brown. The stout branches extended at right angles to the trunk.

"What do you see?" said Morrie.

Nick stepped closer to the wide glass doors. "A tree."

Morrie raised an index finger. "Yes, but what do you *see?*"

Nick didn't reply. Morrie was testing him, and Nick didn't want to sound stupid.

"Contemplate what's in front of you, Nick. Remarkable, isn't it? It reaches down into the ground and up toward the sky and continually branches out at both ends."

Severed Roots

Nick had never thought of a tree in those terms. He continued gazing at the red oak for a long time, while Morrie waited in silence. Soon, the branches of the tree reminded Nick of human arms, and the trunk of a human torso, a robust human torso.

Nick said, "I see a human being."

"Bravo, my boy!" Morrie's face lit up. "Now reflect—a tree's roots branch out and intertwine below the surface, supporting the tree and keeping it upright, even in a heavy wind."

Nick nodded.

Morrie turned and faced Nick squarely. "It's the same for people—our strength depends on our roots."

Nick nodded again, trying to hold on to that idea. *Our strength depends on our roots.* As they returned to the table, he sucked in a quick breath. Where were *his* roots?

Soon Hannah and Rebecca brought in the entrée—Italian eggplant lasagna—accompanied by a heavenly aroma of garlic, tomatoes and ground beef. Nick helped himself to an extra-large portion. The salty cheese melted on his tongue, complementing the tanginess and sponginess of the eggplant. Nick's heart warmed.

"How did you manage to have children? I mean—"

"This"—Morrie displayed the Rite of Passage tattoo on the back of his right hand—"almost destroyed my will to live. Fortunately, I chanced upon a way to reverse the effects of the chemicals, to restore my sex drive and fertility. Unfortunately," he said with a wink at Nick, "I can't tell you more, or I'd have to kill you."

Nick's skin prickled from head to toe. Reversing the effects of the Rite of Passage was a serious crime, an existential threat to the New World Order. He took a deep breath. "Are you...affiliated with the Hardinians?"

CHAPTER THIRTEEN

"No," snapped Morrie. "The Hardinians are violent and have a distorted view of family, of parental rights and responsibilities."

The knot in Nick's stomach eased. Morrie disapproved of violence. Whatever he and Hanna were up to couldn't be too bad. Maybe he shouldn't rush to report them to the authorities until he learned more about them.

Just as he hadn't informed on Beatrice for discarding her Ministry-issued medication.

He turned to Hanna, who was bringing a forkful of lasagna to her lips. "Are you happy, y'know, being a... umm...mother?"

Hanna's fork paused midair. "Yes." She smiled. "I'm also happy being a doctor—I work at Ottawa General. But my first priority is my family."

Nick frowned. *This is too bizarre.* He reached for the pitcher of water in the centre of the table. Across from him, Daniel, the younger boy, was poking his food with a fork.

"Nick," Hanna continued, "family is the best system for transmitting good values to the next generation. I'm helping to create a more wholesome society."

The table lurched slightly. Nick caught sight of Daniel. A strange fire burned in the boy's eyes and his lower lip trembled.

Morrie leaned forward. "What's wrong, son?"

Daniel scrunched up his face. He let out a whine and kicked the leg of the table.

"Why are you upset, Daniel?" Morrie asked, drawing his bushy eyebrows together.

Daniel kicked again, harder, rattling the china.

Hanna took over. "You feel angry. It's okay to feel angry. But it's not okay to kick things. Please stop."

Daniel continued kicking, though not as hard.

Nick stole a look at the other children. They were eyeing Daniel calmly. Did this kind of disturbance happen frequently? Twisting the napkin between his damp fingers, he fervently hoped Morrie and Hanna wouldn't hurt the child. History class had taught him that parents controlled their possessions by yelling at them, cursing them, beating them.

"Daniel," Hanna said in a soft yet firm voice. "I'm going to count to five, and if you don't stop kicking the table, you will have to leave the room."

"One...two...three..." She took a slow breath and continued, "Four." Daniel stopped kicking, buried his face in the crook of his arm and began crying. Nick let out the breath he'd been holding and watched Hanna get up and walk over to the boy. As she put her arm around Daniel's shoulders, Nick blinked rapidly, taking it all in. "Thank you for listening, Danny."

Hanna stood for a long time, hugging her son while everyone else watched. When the crying stopped, Morrie spoke. "If you want to tell Mommy or Daddy what's bothering you, we're happy to listen. Whenever you're ready, that is."

Daniel lifted his head and turned his tearful eyes on Morrie. Then he glanced at Nick and at everyone else around the table.

"I hate eggplant." His voice was barely audible. "It's yucky."

"Oh, that's right. I forgot, honey." Hanna's gaze bounced off Morrie's face and landed back on her son. "I wanted to prepare an Italian dish for our honoured guest, and I thought he might like eggplant. You don't have to eat it, but you still need to finish the rest of the lasagna. And then, well, if you ask politely, you may get some extra dessert."

Daniel swallowed hard. "What's for dessert?"

"It's a secret for now," said Hanna. "But I know you'll love it. You can help Becky bring it out when we're all done eating."

Daniel nodded. The conversation turned to worldly matters: the similarities and differences between Italian and Spanish cuisine; the Advisor's reelection platform, in particular her promise to narrow the meaning of "defamation" in order to allow for freer expression in the arts and in political discourse. This was followed by an interesting exercise whereby each person around the table was invited to share something they were grateful for. Morrie had kicked it off by relating how much he had learned about magic from Nick in just three weeks. Hanna was thankful for her family's good health and togetherness. When it was Nick's turn, he'd expressed gratitude for having Morrie as a friend. The kids were appreciative of their large house, caring parents, "a ton of toys" and delicious food.

Nick felt good about the activity, though he couldn't pinpoint why.

As soon as Daniel's plate contained only eggplant and everyone else had finished eating, he got up and followed his older sister out of the room. A few minutes later, they brought out the dessert—vanilla ice cream with strawberry sauce and nut topping—to the delighted squeals of their siblings.

Nick positioned his bowl of dessert directly in front of him and licked his lips.

"Nick, we wanted you to have a taste of family," Morrie piped up. "As you can see, families are like ice cream—mostly sweet with a few nuts."

Everyone laughed, including Daniel.

"Seriously, though, many families throughout history have been dysfunctional," Hanna said, between spoonfuls.

"Um, isn't that why they've been outlawed?" Nick asked. "So why...?"

"Right. But that doesn't mean the institution of the family is flawed, only that it demands effort and skills for it to work."

Nick stopped eating and rested a fist against his forehead, deep in thought. *Morrie and Hanna used a gentle but firm method to address their son's misbehaviour.* He scratched his chin and reflected on a storybook a facilitator at the Children's Centre had often read to the boys, featuring Mr. Makeright, a hunched-over, angry father who would pull out his leather belt and flog his possessions—a three-year-old boy and a five-year-old girl—each time they neglected to put away their toys. And he reflected on his own experience in the Children's Centre, where the facilitators administered drugs to calm the unruly children, including him.

After dessert, Morrie insisted Nick join the children in the playroom while he and Hanna cleared the table and set up for tea. The room was accessible via a trapdoor in the kitchen floor.

As Nick descended into the playroom, he was dazzled by the brightness, the colourfully patterned walls and floor and the countless toys filling the area. *A fantasy place.*

The children squabbled over which game to play; London Bridge, Create-a-Story, and relay races were a few of the suggestions.

"Why don't we ask our guest?" said Rebecca.

As they looked at Nick, his mouth went dry, and his palms became sweaty. He hadn't played with children since his days at the Children's Centre, over sixteen years ago. The children looked around nervously, as if trying to locate something appropriate for a grown-up. Everyone except Nathalie, the youngest child. She marched to the lower shelf of a bookcase and pulled out a small white container.

"Sir, do you know how to play jackstraws?"

Nick hesitated. "'Fraid I never heard of it."

"Oh, it's really fun," said Nathalie, as she picked at the edges of the plastic cover. "We'll teach you."

No one objected. Rebecca explained the goal was to fish out the jackstraws with your fingers one at a time without making the others move, even by a hair's breadth. If any other jackstraw moved, it would be the next person's turn.

"And the colour is important," Stephen added. "Yellow ones are worth three points, reds are five, blues are ten, greens are fifteen, and the white one is worth twenty."

"That's right," said Rebecca. "At the end, we each add up all the points from the sticks we took out. The player with the highest score wins."

They gathered around the table. "Let Mr. Wong start. He's the oldest," said Danny.

"I should start," Nathalie protested, nostrils flaring. "I'm the youngest."

"So what?" Stephen said. "I'm the middle-est."

"Actually, I think I'd better go first," Rebecca said, taking the box from Nathalie. "So I can show Mr. Wong how to play." She mixed the sticks in her hands, bunched them up and, holding them above the tabletop, allowed them to collapse in a haphazard pile. She took a few minutes to study the layout before picking up the safer ones, gradually proceeding to the more challenging ones. She collected a few sticks before inadvertently causing a green one to move.

Nick was next. He was still reflecting on the fact that the children addressed him as Mr. Wong—something he was not used to but for some reason liked hearing—as he removed a yellow stick, then a blue one. Nathalie squealed in delight. Everyone rooted for him as he reached with his thumb and index finger for the white stick, which was partially entrapped between a yellow and a green one.

Nick mustered the powers of concentration he used while performing his magic tricks. He made himself completely oblivious to his surroundings. He pictured his hand as the hand of a surgeon.

He succeeded in freeing the white stick, and immediately there were cheers and clapping. "Got it!" Nick punched the air in triumph. He then removed two yellow sticks fairly easily but failed on the green one.

Daniel was next. He moved like a sloth, while Nathalie rolled her eyes. He freed four sticks but fell short on the next attempt. He slammed a fist into the palm of his other hand in frustration.

When it was Nathalie's turn, Daniel and Stephen were already quietly adding up their scores, as if they didn't think a five-year-old could win. Twice, Nathalie caused another jackstraw to move slightly, but the other children didn't notice. No, they *must* have noticed. They were being nice, giving her a break.

Nick studied the children—Rebecca's sunny disposition, Stephen's gracious eyes, Daniel's Mona Lisa smile, Nathalie's assertive pumpkin face. A mere two hours ago, these children didn't know he existed, and now they were laughing and playing with him. The feeling he had was strange, unfamiliar. He felt warm and protected. A bond of sorts had formed between them.

Severed Roots

It was Rebecca's turn again. Watching her shiny black hair dancing and swaying over the jackstraws, a delightful memory formed in Nick's head. He must have been four or five, before he lived in the Children's Centre. A girl with dark hair, who was a little bigger than he, had taken hold of his hand. Together they'd run, barefoot, across a wide lawn, toward a playground.

She ran faster, pulling him along. When they were three-quarters of the way there, Nick broke into a sprint, squinting against the brilliance of the sun. Soon he pulled *her* and she fell. He stopped and turned around.

Looking up at him and breathing hard, she asked if he could help her up. She'd scraped her knee, and it was covered with a thin layer of dirt, but it wasn't bleeding. Nick knew she could get up by herself, but it felt good to be asked for help. He moved close, reached under her arms and gently helped her stand. They walked in silence the rest of the way to the spring rocking horses, hand in hand.

"Do your children ever leave the house?" Nick said later in the dining room, after an unsuccessful attempt to sip the boiling hot chamomile tea Morrie had brought him.

Morrie took his time chewing a gingerbread cookie while looping and unlooping his thin index finger through the handle of his mug. He glanced at Hanna, Rebecca and Stephen seated at the table. The three were eyeing him. Daniel and Nathalie were still in the basement, playing.

"Whenever we feel suicidal," Morrie laughed. He brought the cup to his lips and took a cautious sip. "I don't want my kids to feel like they're in prison, so sometimes we play hockey outside. We were caught once, and fortunately I was able to pay off the bureaucrat. Talk about making good use of my boundless wealth." Morrie laughed again, this time nervously. "Since then, I've been picked up and questioned twice. I'm afraid if we're caught again, the children will be seized, and I'll end up behind bars. I wouldn't be able to continue my important work."

"What's that?"

Morrie looked at Nick intently for a few seconds. He cleared his throat and spoke slowly. "I work for an underground organization whose goal is to recruit young people to get married and start families."

"Young people?"

"Like you and Beatrice."

Nick's face warmed. He looked into his mug of tea, deep in thought. He pressed a fist to his lips. "I thought you were a real friend." His voice trembled. "You tricked me."

"Aha! I tricked the magician!" Morrie laughed. "You must be proud of your student!"

Nick glowered at him.

Morrie shifted in his chair. "Look, Nick. What's a friend, if not someone who cares about you and wants the best for you?"

Nick flinched. A strange coldness hit him at the core. He turned to Morrie and slammed an open hand on the table, causing the cookie plate to jump. The children recoiled. "You made up this story about wanting to learn magic so you could befriend me and brainwash me with your ideology!"

"Nick, I'm not going to lie to you abou—"

"You've already lied to me!" He pushed his chair out. "I bet you made up the whole story about your pneumonia, too, and got me totally drenched for no good reason." Nick was still for a moment, then cupped a hand over his eyes. "How—how could you?"

"I'm sorry. *Extremis malis, extrema remedia.* You've no idea what we're up against. I put my trust in you, Nick—"

"Trust? You *used* me, Morrie. You took advantage of me and deceived me."

"Nick, listen to me." Morrie thrust an index finger at him. "This is a secret organization. I'm taking a big risk. You can easily report me. Then my family, my wife, my kids will be ruined."

Rebecca spoke from the edge of the room, her voice quivering, "Mr. Wong, we're *happy* here. Please, *please* don't tell on us. They'll take us away..."

Rebecca's eyes brimmed with tears. Just like Beatrice's, crying in Amazon Mall. Nick stared down at the floor, his anger easing.

"Nick," Morrie said softly. "I've taken a big chance on you, and I'm prepared to take an even bigger one—because I believe in you, in your goodness. I'm confident you'll see that the goals of our organization are moral. I want to tell you how we operate. But it's late, and we're all tired. You'll sleep here tonight, in one of the bedrooms upstairs, and tomorrow morning we'll continue our discussion."

Nick felt as though he were falling into an abyss. He wanted to go home, to think by himself. It occurred to him that if he were to refuse Morrie's offer, Morrie and Hanna might force him to stay, perhaps tie him up, even shoot him.

Nick broke into a cold sweat. Morrie's friendship had been a ruse, and there was no telling what he'd do now. Nick needed to show he was strong, unafraid; he also needed to avoid provoking Morrie to do anything rash.

"I need to get away to think," Nick said. "And I need my migraine pills, or my head will explode. I have to go home."

Morrie watched him silently, while Hanna's face tightened. Nick looked at the floor. He checked that his shoelaces were not loose in case he'd need to dash for the door. He began to get up.

Before Nick was fully upright, Stephen, who had positioned himself near Nick and barely reached his shoulders, pushed him back into his chair. "You're not going anywhere unless you promise you won't tell on us. And if you break your promise, my father will kill you. He has killed before, many times."

"Stephen!" Morrie jumped up and grabbed his son's arm. "Go to your room this instant." To Nick he said, "I'm so sorry. He threatened you because he's afraid of what might happen."

"Of course, of course," Nick said, shaking inside. "I'm interested in learning about your organization. But I do need my medication, or my head will burst. You can come by my place tomorrow morning, and we'll talk more." Nick stood up again, slowly, and inched toward the doorway.

Morrie followed Nick into the living room. As they passed the grand piano, Morrie said, "Not so fast." They were both in the middle of the room, and the adjoining den was in full view.

Nick halted and turned to Morrie. Morrie glanced back at Hanna, then peered through the doorway connected to the den, where the firearm lay exposed on the coffee table. His eyes gleamed, and a strange cryptic expression spread across his hairy face, a mix of gravity and impishness. He took two steps toward the den, then stopped, appearing to have changed his mind. He turned his attention back to Nick.

"Okay, my friend. Tomorrow morning. First thing."

CHAPTER FOURTEEN

The bus ride was a blur. Nick arrived home still shaking and grabbed a half-finished can of pop from the kitchen counter. After washing down the pills his doctor had prescribed, he staggered to his mattress on the floor and collapsed.

He stared at the ceiling, faintly illuminated by light from the window. *How does Morrie's family escape exposure and punishment? True, their house is at the end of a cul-de-sac, obscured by enormous trees. But still.*

And the kids? They seem happy, but beneath that veneer they must be scarred by family life...mustn't they? And surely they live in constant fear of being caught. Are there other such clandestine families in the city?

Nick tried to let go of his tumultuous thoughts, but they refused to leave. How dare Morrie try to ensnare him into endorsing that kind of lifestyle? How dare he pretend to be doing it for Nick's benefit? And what had possessed him to let Morrie come by tomorrow? What was he going to do when his phony friend showed up?

Nego Huzcotoq

He rubbed his forehead, willing himself to relax. The pills slowly began to ease the tension in his head. Eventually, sleep overtook him.

Rapid knocking broke into Nick's heavy sleep. He froze under his blanket. Morrie's booming voice penetrated the thin door.

"Nick! Open up, my friend."

Morrie was much smaller than Nick, but he was agile, and he might have his gun. He might even have brought an accomplice.

Nick reached for his clock and squinted at the red numbers: 4:46 a.m. *Does that guy never sleep?*

"Nick, let me in. We agreed last night!" The knocking became louder, more insistent, and alternated with a rattling of the door handle.

Nick's heartbeat thrashed in his ears. He decided to stay put, needing time to figure out what to do. Morrie had lied to him, betrayed his trust, and he was capable of doing so again.

After what seemed like an eternity, the banging and rattling stopped, as did Morrie's entreaties to open the door. Nick considered staying inside the entire day. But Morrie could return the next day. Or the day after. Nick refused to be a prisoner in his own home.

Severed Roots

He needed to stand up like a woman and make some decisions.

Truth is a friend that never betrays. Beatrice's words came to him, and he whispered them over and over. Sitting up, he pushed his blanket onto the floor and swung his legs around.

He knew what he had to do.

Morrie drew several deep breaths as he walked briskly along the vacant streets away from Nick's home. The predawn air was refreshing, helping to calm his nerves.

He's avoiding me, taking refuge in a hole in the ground. A stuffy, mouldy hole in the ground.

Like a mole.

Morrie's shadow waxed and waned as he moved through the yellow pools of the streetlights. He had misjudged Nick. Nick's selfless act in the bus during that rainstorm had skewed Morrie's perception of him. Altruism was not the same as openness to new ideas. Or maybe the fact that Nick was a magician—his world was a dance between reality and illusion—had made Morrie foolishly believe Nick would see the emptiness and falsehood of this society.

Yet Morrie had always been an excellent judge of character. That skill had kept him alive all this time. He couldn't have gotten this one so wrong. Reexamining one's worldview took time; that was all.

Morrie hoped to arrive home while the streetlights were still illuminated. As he walked, he imagined the long shadows cast by his small frame provided protection from any potential predators. Once home, he would consult with Hanna and strategize what to do about Nick.

The faint slam of a car door startled him, jarring his frayed nerves. He glanced about and picked up his pace, chiding himself for leaving his gun at home. True, he hadn't wanted to risk scaring Nick, but Morrie had a habit of being too sure of himself. One day he'd pay for this failing.

A block away, the silhouettes of two people appeared from an alley. Morrie slowed. At first, he couldn't determine whether the figures were walking toward or away from him, but soon the matter became clear.

Morrie's blood ran cold. Two men in hoodies stood on the sidewalk, partly facing each other, evidently waiting for him to approach. His shoulders shuddered.

Okay, I mustn't show I'm afraid. I'll walk right past them, even say Good morning.

As the figures grew larger and more distinct, fear gave way to terror. Morrie's heart raced.

Severed Roots

"Well, if it ain't our simian friend," the taller man called out with a Spanish accent. "Heading back to da zoo, *supongo*?"

Morrie slowed his gait, both as a prudent display of politeness and because his path was blocked. "Hi, Pablo, Mitchel. Sorry. No time to chat. My wife's expecting me back—"

"A monkey dat leeves een a palace. Da zookeeper must be wealthy. Of course—da wife's a *doctor*. Good for her. Mitch, let's give da good lady some beezness, shall we?"

Pablo grabbed Morrie's right wrist and jerked it sharply toward himself. With his other hand on Morrie's short-sleeved upper arm, he drove his knee upward against the back of Morrie's elbow.

Morrie howled and staggered backward, grasping his upper arm with his left hand. Searing pain radiated throughout his body. He fell, his buttocks landing on the hard pavement. Mitchel squatted beside him and looked him in the eyes.

"We gave you many chances. We would have gladly welcomed you back."

Morrie squirmed, aghast, at the jagged, bloody bone protruding from the skin near his elbow.

"Do you think you can hide behind that thick beard, Morrie George?" Mitchel continued, his voice softer. "We know what you've been doing. Prostituting yourself to the government in exchange for the freedom to live like a king, with—how many little ones now? Four? Five?" Mitchel thrust an index finger into the air. "Mark my words, the Hardinian revolution will succeed."

"I'm n-not a threat," Morrie stammered in agony.

Mitchel curled his lip into a sneer. "No? How long since you defected? Five years? Hard to believe, eh? You were a real danger to us then, a storehouse of intelligence. Now you're a nuisance. A bug to squash when we're in the mood."

Morrie pushed himself to his feet, still clutching his arm, blood bubbling up and dripping onto the pavement.

"You see, my old amigo," Pablo added, "last night, one of our best hideouts was raided—da one behind Dixie Bridge. Remember dat one? It makes us wonder how da government knew…"

"I had nothing to do with it!" Morrie staggered backward a few steps, eyes darting between the jeering faces of his tormentors. Seeing they remained in place, he turned himself around, his whole body trembling, and half ran, half stumbled in the direction of his home, with the dignity of a confused, wounded animal.

"*Hasta luego*, my old *amigo*," Pablo called out. "Until da next time."

CHAPTER FIFTEEN

Karla looked down from the twentieth-floor window of the Ministry building and watched a dozen human bodies in the front parking lot wither and shrivel, becoming one blackened, charred heap. Plumes of smoke rose and sullied the blue sky. *Oh please, dear God, not again.* She pushed her ear to the window glass and closed her eyes. A loudspeaker crackled and came to life.

"Let the Ministry officials, the Canadian government and the World Federation take note. Our message is as clear as the flames before you and as strong as the smell of burning flesh. The lonely life is not worth living."

Karla retreated from the glass, her chest tightening. *These self-immolations are now almost weekly.* She pulled the curtain closed, leaned her back against it and whimpered. After a while, she plodded back to her leather swivel chair and sat.

She stared across her desk at the ocean mural and waited for Nick to arrive. A pod of bottlenose dolphins jumped and twirled amid colourful water creatures, from seahorses and puffer fish to coral and sea anemones.

Secretly, Karla had always likened herself to a dolphin, a gentle inhabitant of the waters, carrying herself with poise and grace. Dolphins, apart from being the most intelligent creatures in the great oceans, were compassionate. They often stayed with people who were injured or sick and even helped them breathe by bringing them to the surface.

But today she didn't feel dolphin-like. She gazed at the curtain and felt a pain in the back of her throat. She'd done nothing for the world, for humanity. There was so much suffering, so much loneliness, so much dissent, and she just sat at her mahogany desk day after day, year after year, poring over documents and getting older.

Two days had passed since Morrie banged on Nick's apartment door. Fortunately, Morrie had not returned the following day or tried to contact him. And happily, Karla had informed Nick his new job would start today.

Nick's apprehension about working in a government office and reporting to Karla was tempered by a burning determination to learn everything he could about the Ministry's ideology. He could then assess Morrie's aberrant lifestyle and know whether he should reconnect with him or—ouch!—report him and Hanna to the authorities.

As he rode up the elevator, he stood tall, facing the wall mirror, gazing at the blue collared shirt and charcoal dress pants he'd bought for this occasion. The outfit, he fantasized, gave him the confidence of a woman. He smiled. *I'm on a mission.*

Five minutes later, Nick was shown to Karla's office, where she welcomed him with a firm handshake and reminded him that she headed the research branch.

"Our main interest is helping women who suffer from motherhood syndrome—or MS—like your friend Beatrice. It's a condition that makes them clinically depressed, but we're hoping to turn them back into productive members of society."

Nick leaned forward in his chair.

"It's interesting to note the different attitudes toward MS," Karla continued. "Most sufferers seek treatment. But others—a minority—see nothing wrong with motherhood syndrome, and some attempt to have a baby, knowing full well they could end up in jail." Karla waved a hand. "Of course, we don't get involved in the legal side of things in this branch, only the research. My boss does get involved, though.

She's chief of enforcement for the entire country. She's ruthless."

Ruthless? A shiver ran up Nick's spine.

Karla leaned back in her swivel chair and placed her forearms on the armrests. "By the way, she told me she'd drop in later to meet you."

Nick sat up straighter and adjusted his collar. Why would Karla's boss want to meet him? And on his first day on the job. Protocol?

"What's her name?"

Karla smiled smugly. "Doreeta. But she doesn't let anyone call her that, except me. Everyone else calls her Dr. Stone."

Nick frowned. "What will my duties be?"

"Obviously, you don't have any research skills. Dor—Dr. Stone—knows that. For now, we mostly want to tap into your perspective as a nonwoman. There are no mankeys in this branch, except for a few clerks."

Karla rose from her chair and led Nick out the door. She walked him to the opposite end of the narrow corridor, past a Miss Muffins coffee maker, and showed him his office.

The room was the size of his basement apartment and spotless, with a bare grey desk, two ergonomic pivot chairs and a metal filing cabinet that held pictures of the current and past Advisors, as well as a statuette of the Goddess of Liberty. They were the same portraits and statuette he'd seen in Karla's more ostentatious office.

He'd never had an office before, and he felt both important and clueless. Karla asked Nick to spend the rest of the afternoon accessing files from a computer database and familiarizing himself with sample survey questionnaires. "The questionnaires," Karla said before she left, "are aimed at motherhood syndrome sufferers. They relate to the nature, intensity and duration of their symptoms."

A few minutes later, a knock came at the door. Nick looked up from his monitor. Karla stood in the doorway, accompanied by a stocky middle-aged woman with a double chin, her thin black hair pulled back in a bun.

The two were holding hands.

"Our future is near! So, you're our new *consultant*," said the stocky woman, dropping Karla's hand and taking a few steps forward. "A pleasure to meet you. My name is Dr. Stone. Karla has told me a lot about you." She spoke in spurts and seemed to have difficulty breathing.

Nick rose. "Our future is near! I hope I can be useful."

"Don't worry. We will make *very* good use of you," she said, winking at Karla. "We do extremely important work. Canada is the leading country in the Federation's

R&D on treatment modalities for motherhood syndrome. All eyes are on us."

Nick's armpits felt hot and clammy. He forced a casual smile. "I'll do my best."

Dr. Stone nodded. "I'm sure you'll benefit from Karla's mentorship and her—ah—*special relationship* with you. And now, if you'll excuse me, I must return to my responsibilities. Our future is near!"

She and Karla turned to leave. Pondering what she'd meant by "special relationship," Nick also wondered about the contraption on Dr. Stone's back. Two inflated vinyl sacks were strapped to her shoulder blades, and a long tube disappeared above the top of her violet pants. *A device to help her breathe?*

He returned to his monitor and began reading the latest version of the questionnaires.

> *What time of day is your pain most acute?*
> *1. Morning*
> *2. Afternoon*
> *3. Evening*
> *4. Night*

He glanced around. His office was bland. Metallic. Geometric. Karla's office at least had a colourful mural.

Severed Roots

How would you describe the pain?
1. Physical only
2. Physical and emotional.
3. Emotional only

Nick stifled a yawn. What was the purpose of his reading these survey questions? Being a mankey, he couldn't relate to any of them.

How many times a day do you think about babies?
1. One to five times
2. Five to twenty times
3. Over twenty times

Karla gazed at her reflection in the shiny filing cabinet. She liked looking at herself that way, because the poor quality of the reflection hid her premature wrinkles and the white hairs recently showing up on her head. A few minutes earlier, she'd returned from a meeting with Doreeta where she had felt self-conscious about her appearance.

Nick burst into her office, jarring Karla from her contemplation.

Swallowing her annoyance, she made a mental note to coach him on workplace etiquette.

"I don't get it," Nick blurted. "Haven't women throughout history wanted babies?" Nick's voice was louder than it needed to be. "Wasn't it an evolutionary necessity? Otherwise our species would have died out."

"Excellent questions," Karla said, her eyes still focused on the filing cabinet. "People think in the Age of Oppression all women wanted babies, which is a myth. Most women had babies against their will, due to their husband's irrepressible libido." Karla sighed. The image on the filing cabinet looked sad and tired. "And for weeks after the birth, they'd suffer from sleeping difficulties, irritability, sadness, concentration problems. There was a name for it—postpartum depression.

"In any case," Karla continued, looking at Nick as she warmed to the subject, "even if something is natural, that doesn't mean it's right. Our purpose in this world is to transcend our nature, not surrender to it."

Nick furrowed his brow.

"The point is this," Karla said. "Now that we've evolved beyond the need for family units, MS is a pathological condition. There are, as I mentioned earlier, two types. The mild cases—those who just fantasize about becoming a mother. And the more serious cases—those who would pursue extreme measures to fulfill their craving."

"What do they do?"

"Many go to the Island Houses."

"The Island Houses?"

Karla admired Nick's curiosity. She waved him to an empty chair. Nick sat.

"They're not actually on islands, but we call them Island Houses because they are, generally speaking, isolated enclaves where much of the clandestine activity takes place."

Nick winced.

Karla suppressed a smile. She knew the mere mention of the word *clandestine* would have an effect on him. Deception bothered Nick. And to think he was a magician.

"Have you ever been to one?" Nick asked, a little too pointedly.

"To an Island House?" Karla arched her eyebrows. "Nick, if we knew where these places were located, we'd raid them in an instant." She half wished Nick would drop the subject. On the other hand, he did need to be trained. Educated. Molded. She raised her voice a notch. "We do know MS cases find their way to these places in search of a male partner who's never been treated in order to procreate. They usually end up living there and producing baby after baby. It's quite disgusting."

Nick stared at Karla for a long time, saying nothing. Karla's stomach hardened. She saw in Nick's frown an intense inquisitiveness, and for the first time, that scared her.

CHAPTER SIXTEEN

Over the next two weeks, Nick worked for Karla on Tuesdays and Thursdays. He brought morning and afternoon coffee to the senior managers, a task he pretended to enjoy. He also read through survey questions and made comments in the margins, although he had little to contribute. Nick suspected Karla had nothing of substance for him to do and just kept him there so he could make money and feel good about himself.

Nick didn't mind. He was behind on his rent. And while—*ugh*—he still hadn't gotten around to visiting Angelina in Franklin House, it wouldn't be right to take money from a dying woman.

Besides, he liked having an office. The furniture, despite its drab colour, smelled new and inviting.

At times, Nick was tempted to tell Karla about Morrie. Morrie hadn't tried making any contact since his early morning knocking on Nick's door, so Nick was probably out of danger. But he shouldn't let

Morrie get away with continued criminal activity. Karla's boss, as chief of enforcement, would want to know, and Karla would be grateful if Nick disclosed the information.

But every time he geared himself up to broach the subject, he was stopped by the memory of Morrie's children, so happy together. If he blew the whistle, they would be taken away and separated from one another. A shudder always followed that thought as another image rose in his mind: the shiny gun resting on the glass-top coffee table in Morrie's den.

What in the world is that gun for?

Nick pushed himself away from the computer monitor, closed his door, and paced back and forth in his office, deep in thought.

Morrie was a small man with a cheerful countenance—not the type one would normally consider dangerous—but he was odd and unpredictable and had a lot to lose if Nick were to betray him. And his son Stephen sounded dead serious when he said Morrie had killed before.

Could he confide in Karla? He stopped pacing and set his eyes on the maple-coloured mug next to his computer monitor: "AN OUNCE OF FRIENDSHIP IS WORTH MORE THAN A POUND OF BLOOD" and "I WILL ALWAYS BE YOUR FRIEND—KARLA ROOK," read the inscription. Nick frowned. Karla had never told

Severed Roots

Nick why she had offered him a job. Maybe she had a less-than-altruistic motivation for employing Nick. Maybe she hoped to educate—brainwash?—him in the Ministry's ideology and ensure his loyalty to her.

If so, then Karla had a hidden agenda and was no better than Morrie. That wasn't good. Nick needed to be extra vigilant. He must never stop questioning... everything.

One afternoon, a rap sounded on Nick's open office door. Karla stood in the entrance, her eyes sparkling with resolve.

"Come with me, Nick. It's time I showed you our clinic."

A clinic? Nick perked up. Finally, something different from the dreary computer work he'd been assigned.

Nick followed Karla down two long hallways to a room marked Outpatient. She tapped the door and opened it.

The room was sparsely furnished. The air felt unusually warm and oozed a peaches-and-cream fragrance. Three young women in flower-print gowns looked up, eyes widened, as Karla and Nick entered. They were seated on wooden chairs in different corners of the room. Each one held a limp, diapered infant on her lap.

"Just showing the new employee around," Karla announced. "Pardon our intrusion."

Nick locked eyes with the woman closest to him. She had high cheekbones and arched eyebrows beneath wavy, strawberry-blond hair. She slowly twisted her upper body, revealing the baby's head. Nick gasped. The infant had grotesque bulging eyes and a scaly reddish-brown growth the size of a golf ball on its scalp.

"This is Clarisse," said Karla, gesturing toward the woman. "Over there is Nicole, and this lady to our left is Ruah."

Ruah leaned back in her chair, arms stretched out and holding her baby stiffly on the edge of her lap. Nick stepped back, his eyes widening. This baby was deformed too. It had two holes in lieu of a nose. Large, shapeless pieces of flesh hung on either side of its head where there should have been ears.

Nick's eyes darted to Nicole. She was looking down at her infant and quietly sobbing. A stump instead of an arm extended from one of the infant's shoulders. Nick shuddered.

"These are brave women, Nick," Karla declared in a loud voice. "All three have been seeking treatment."

Nick tore his gaze away from Nicole and peered into Karla's steady grey eyes.

"Clarisse did not respond well to taking anti-depressants because of the side effects. For Nicole and Ruah, pharmacotherapy proved helpful but insufficient. So all three of these amazing women are undergoing an innovative form of therapy."

Nick felt hot and light-headed. "Why–why are the babies deformed...and lifeless?"

Karla smiled. "What we do here is ask the patient to close her eyes and imagine she's just given birth and is about to be handed her new baby. We encourage her to say out loud, in the greatest detail, what the baby looks like—its angelic face, its tiny fingers, its shiny eyes. We instruct the patient to imagine how it feels to hold the 'bundle of joy'—the warmth of the baby's body, the soft breath, the kicking legs, the divine smell. Then, after the patient has finished describing her imagined experience, we instruct her to open her eyes, and immediately we hand her one of these newborns."

Nick crinkled his nose.

"The patients are to cradle the babies for as long as they can bear it. When they can no longer endure, they walk over to that wall and press the green button. A nurse enters. She helps the patient to carefully place the baby in one of those bins, marked Refuse, and carries the bin out of the room."

Nick's head was spinning. His legs trembled.

"Don't worry," said Karla, taking a step toward Nick. "These babies are actually reused. And they're not dead. We anaesthetize them before giving them to the women. Studies show the sound of babies crying elicits empathy, which would be counterproductive for the therapy. These babies are in no way harmed. And, as I said, all our patients are willing participants. They really want to overcome their MS."

The wave of nausea that had swirled through Nick's stomach slowly subsided. "Does the therapy work?"

"Sometimes. There's no guarantee. If it doesn't work, the next step is usually psychosurgery."

"What's that?" Nick's pulse quickened. He realized he'd been practically holding his breath. He forced himself to exhale and take in new air, air that was too heavy, too thick.

"It's not pleasant. It involves drilling into the skull and burning an area of the brain responsible for compulsive emotions." Karla tilted her head at Nick. "I know all this seems cruel, Nick. But we must do everything we can to eradicate this illness. Am I right, ladies?"

The women nodded almost imperceptibly, their eyes glued to their assigned infants.

"May you be cured speedily, ladies," Karla said. She placed a hand behind Nick's back and nudged him toward the exit.

As they reached the door, one of the women began to sob. Nick and Karla turned around.

"But..."

"Yes, Ruah?" Karla said.

Ruah was looking up. Her roundish face, streaked with tears, conjured a memory of Beatrice crying on the bench in Amazon Mall. "This is not my baby. *My* baby would not look like this."

"Can you be sure, Ruah? In procreation, there are no guarantees. You get what you get." And with a wave of dismissal, Karla swiveled to face the exit.

Nick accompanied Karla a few steps down the hall, then grabbed her forearm.

Karla froze, wide-eyed. "Nick, what—"

"Where are they from?"

"What?"

"I want to know where those babies are from." Nick spoke forcefully, tightening his grip.

Karla was silent for a moment and then laughed. "Nick, did you think we manufacture deformed babies for the therapy? Are you worried you might be living in some dystopian reality? Those are accidents of nature."

Nick took a step back, releasing his hold on Karla's arm.

"They're mostly from women who get pregnant illegally. The criminals have trouble managing their pregnancies while in hiding—having no access to proper hygiene and medical care—so the fetuses often don't survive or sometimes come out deformed. It's sad, but at least these infants are being put to good use."

"What causes the deformities?"

"Like I said, they're accidents of nature. In theory, it can happen even with our surrogates. The difference is that the criminals, having no access to medical diagnostics, are not aware of the deformities until their babies are born and so don't abort them."

"What happens when those babies grow up?"

"We give them social assistance and encourage some to go on tours to warn people of the dangers of trying to manufacture human products on your own."

They walked the rest of the way to their offices in silence.

Over the next few days, Nick replayed the scene at the clinic. He thought of Beatrice, wondering how she'd react if she gave birth to a deformed baby. *My little angel no matter what,* he could imagine her saying. Or something like that. The Ministry's novel therapy wouldn't work on Beatrice. She'd need psychosurgery.

Severed Roots

One drizzly morning, while parking his bike in front of the stately Ministry building, Nick noticed a woman a hundred feet away, her sleeveless yellow dress fluttering in the wind. She was short and shapely, with shoulder-length blond hair. She stood motionless, her back to him, holding a pail. The woman looked familiar.

As he watched, she carefully raised the pail over her head and tilted it, causing liquid to fall over her hair and down her dress.

In a flash, Nick realized what was happening. His eyes opened wide, and his body shook.

He tried to scream but no sound would come. *Beatrice!* He sprinted toward the woman on trembling legs.

She held a lighter to the bottom of her dress.

His heart raced. "No...!"

The flames licked her yellow dress, her hair. She screamed, circling erratically as the blaze gained momentum and transformed her into a human fireball.

Nick froze in horror and then backed away from the blinding light and intense heat in quick, jerky steps. Dizziness made it hard to stay upright.

He wanted to throw her to the ground and roll around with her to smother the flames, but they would both die.

The woman's face glowed in the orange flames, a look of desperation and defiance. Nick let out a long breath. She was not Beatrice. He held his hands together, holding back tears. *That's Ruah.*

The woman collapsed to her knees and writhed on the ground.

Nick stared at her helplessly, struggling to contain the food in his stomach. Security guards ran out of the nearby building with fire extinguishers. In less than a minute, the flames were out. Moments later, an ambulance braked beside Nick, and attendants carried the charred body away on a stretcher. Nick covered his nose and mouth.

For the remainder of the morning, Nick couldn't concentrate on the survey questionnaires. His stomach churned. The smell of the burning woman lingered, no matter how many times he tried to clear it from his nostrils. Thoughts of the self-immolation plagued him. A life ruined, and she was about Beatrice's age.

Next time it *could* be Beatrice.

Which day in August was Beatrice turning thirty? He didn't know exactly, but the clock was counting down. He needed to get off his oversized butt and do something—*now*.

On his lunch break, Nick left the Ministry building, biked home and rummaged through his magic supplies. Within a few minutes he'd found what he wanted: his microcamera. After returning to his office an hour later, he took a few deep breaths and walked toward Dr. Stone's office with a stack of survey questionnaires tucked under his arm, pretending he was on his way to see Karla.

Must remain cool. Observe without drawing attention.

Dr. Stone's office door was slightly ajar. Her secretary sat in an open cubicle a few feet away, eyes glued to a computer screen.

Every fifteen or twenty minutes, Nick made another trip past Dr. Stone's office, each time clutching different documents or coloured folders. Twice, he walked by without carrying anything, entered a washroom and headed back a few minutes later. On his seventh excursion, the secretary's cubicle was empty. A sign on her desk announced that "the Chief" had stepped out for a meeting, accompanied by the secretary.

Nick approached Dr. Stone's closed office door. Gently biting his lip, he knocked lightly. Nothing. After a few seconds, he pressed down on the door handle. The door was unlocked.

Perfect.

He slowly released the handle without pushing the door open and rushed back to his office to get what he needed.

Five minutes later, Nick walked into Dr. Stone's office. A strong, skunky smell of weed greeted him. His heart pounded as he placed a fresh cup of coffee on her desk. The action would serve as a cover in case someone spotted him. With slight-of-hand agility, he secured the wide-angle microcamera to a picture frame that hung directly behind and above Dr. Stone's swivel chair.

The operation was a huge risk. Anyone in the room could spot the microcamera if they were observant enough. He tried to calm his nerves. A *few hours is all I need.*

Nick's trembling legs carried him down the quiet corridor back to the privacy of his office. Fifty minutes later, the image of Dr. Stone typing on her keyboard appeared on Nick's phone. After replaying and slowing down the video clip several times, he was able to learn her password: IM#TheBOSS. After several more repetitions, he learned her username.

Nick set to work accessing Dr. Stone's files. Within minutes, he found a top-secret "Strategic Communications" document from the World Federation, entitled "The Progressives—A Growing Menace."

> *...This group, calling itself The Progressives, has been growing over the years and has been identified as a significant threat to the New World*

Order. Unlike the Hardinians under Monsieur Francois Hardin, the Progressives are moderate in their ideology and do not espouse violence.

Nick tapped his chin with a finger. Was Morrie a Progressive? He hadn't used that term, although he did say he wasn't affiliated with the Hardinians. But he did have a gun, though presumably to protect himself and his family from—the government?

Nick stared at his keyboard. If the Progressives were a threat to the government, was it because the government couldn't rationalize rooting them out, like they could with the Hardinians, who were openly violent? Were the Progressives involved in any clandestine activities, such as human manufacturing?

Karla had spoken about "isolated enclaves." She'd called them Island Houses.

Nick began searching for information on Island Houses. After two hours, he had found only one entry—Island House Resort, Iowa, USA.

He opened the file. It was empty.

He sank back in his chair. Should he ask Morrie if he knew anything about the Island Houses? He scratched his head. No—every contact with Morrie risked enmeshing himself in that oddball's criminal organization. And if Nick ever betrayed him, Morrie might kill him.

The microcamera! Nick jumped out of his chair. The longer the device stayed there, the greater the chance someone would notice it.

Nick passed by Dr. Stone's office. The secretary sat typing at her desk. She looked up and their eyes met. Her brow wrinkled. Nick nodded and continued walking nonchalantly to the washroom, sweat dripping from his armpits.

At six thirty, after the secretary had left for the day, he approached Dr. Stone's door again. He grabbed the handle. The door was locked.

Nick's skin tingled. He returned to his desk, undid the top two buttons of his shirt and tried to think. Today was Thursday. He worked for Karla only on Tuesdays and Thursdays. That meant there was a good chance the camera would be discovered before he'd have any chance of removing it. And then, the police would merely have to inspect the area for fingerprints...

My God, what have I done!

He needed to flee. But where to?

He closed his eyes. In his mind, a yellow dress fluttered in the wind. Then the eerie stillness of that woman—Ruah—before she'd set herself on fire. Would she have done that to herself if she'd known about the Island Houses? And Beatrice? When the hell was her birthday? She would soon turn thirty and could follow in Ruah's footsteps. He had to find an Island House before it was too late.

For Beatrice's sake.

Nick's legs were restless. He swung them side to side, trying to calm them—and himself. What if, for whatever reason, Beatrice wouldn't go to live in an Island House? Was it even right for him to try to lead her to an illegal place? He tilted his head, contemplating, then banged a fist on his thigh. *No, I must go there, not only for Beatrice but also for myself. To uncover the truth. Truth is a friend that never betrays.*

Nick sprang to his feet, strode down the vacant corridor and marched into Karla's office—she always worked late. "I won't be in next week. I have two magic performances lined up."

Karla looked at him silently.

This was the first time Nick had blatantly lied to a woman, at least in his adult years. He didn't feel bad about it, though. In fact, he felt it was the right thing to do.

●

After Nick left, Karla leaned into her chair and rubbed the back of her neck. It had been a long day. She got up, locked her office door and walked to her window. The city appeared foggy and dismal as she looked upon it from the twentieth floor. A crowd of lonely women in business suits were heading home. How would they spend their evenings? She thought of Doreeta and asked herself for the umpteenth time why she was attracted to that woman. Admittedly, she admired her determination, her intelligence, her *power*. But she didn't appreciate the way Doreeta sometimes toyed with her, mocked her, particularly when they were making love.

The window was hermetically sealed, but Karla was sure she could smell smoke coming through the vents. In recent months, the air outside the Ministry building smelled increasingly like fried or seared beef. *The acrid odor of burnt human flesh.* She shuffled back to her desk and pulled out a photo of Nico at age three and a half and her at age six, sitting together on a rocking horse in a park. Their sunburned faces looked contented. She stared at the photo for a few minutes, then laid her face down on the cool desktop and sobbed.

CHAPTER SEVENTEEN

The train to Des Moines, Iowa, was filled almost to capacity, mostly with women, some of whom were locked in intimate embraces.

Nick stretched his legs across the unoccupied seat next to him. He slept little but felt good. He'd never done anything as bold as deciding to go to Iowa on impulse.

He had few provisions: a leftover cheese sandwich, a large bag of breakfast cereal, pop and half a dozen candy bars, plus a bit of money he'd scraped together by selling some possessions, including his expensive umbrella.

He looked out the window at the passing lush green yards of suburbia.

What in the world had motivated him to throw himself into the unknown like this? He wanted to see an Island House. Talk to the residents. Ask them questions. Get clarity. Maybe he could save Beatrice's life.

Should he have asked Beatrice to join him? No, the journey could be dangerous. Or not successful.

Better that his best friend be safe at home. He could always get her later.

Nick pulled out his phone and retrieved the text message Morrie had sent him two days ago. "I know you are avoiding me, but under no circumstances are you to contact Beatrice. I believe the government is monitoring her. Delete after reading." Nick hadn't replied. He shook his head, hit 'delete' and put the device back into his pocket.

Would the Island House help Beatrice conceive, perhaps provide her with a fertile man? What if she'd already "celebrated" her birthday? Nick shuddered at the thought. And the Island House...was there a possibility it was run by Hardinians? Would they find out he worked for Canada's Ministry of Tomorrow and take him hostage? He'd have to ditch his government ID pass before he entered the place.

Rain began spitting against the window. A flock of geese flew over a factory as it whizzed passed.

He had made a decision and could not turn back. If the camera on Dr. Stone's wall was discovered— Nick's scalp tingled at the thought; not *if* but *when*— the police would be after him in an instant.

"Des Moines Central Station," the train's PA system announced as the train ground to a halt.

The doors opened. Nick grabbed his backpack and green hybrid bike and stepped onto the dirty platform.

Severed Roots

After securing his bike next to the locker rental area, he made his way to the concourse. He took a deep breath. He'd never been so far from home. Looking around, he spotted a familiar sign—Miss Muffins. Grinning, he entered the coffee shop.

Nick rubbed the back of his neck and rolled his shoulders. *Sixteen hours on a train. Too long.* When his turn came, he ordered an extra-large coffee. The smell of cinnamon and cocoa emanated from a snack case on the counter. It was filled with biscotti and pastries. He forced himself to look away. He needed to save the little money he had. He also decided he should try to lose weight. *Really* lose weight—not his pitiful on-and-off attempts over the years. He was on an important mission and needed to be mindful of his health.

He took his coffee to a seat near the exit. Customers brushed past. He brought the cup to his lips. The hot liquid and the smooth, bitter aftertaste revitalized him. Soon his insides warmed. After a half dozen sips, he decided to ask the next person who passed for directions.

As a slim, greasy-haired brunette was about to pass, Nick stuck his arm out. She stopped. But when he opened his mouth, he couldn't find his voice. His heart pounded. *This whole thing is crazy.* She shrugged and continued on.

Nick's coffee was cool by the time he managed to speak to a broad-shouldered woman leading a Golden Retriever. "Please, I'm looking for the Island House."

She narrowed her eyes and led her dog away. Nick wished he could melt into the table, into the floor. He touched his unshaven face and sniffed under his arm. *Whoa. No wonder she didn't stop.* After a minute, he tried again with someone else. She responded with a curt shake of her head. He made another attempt but was met with a gruff response.

Nick had figured he'd find the Island House by asking people in the train station. Random travelers. And locals. Complete strangers. And he was looking for a top-secret place! Was he an ape-brain? If the locals knew the location of the Island House, wouldn't the authorities know it too? And wouldn't they have already shut the place down?

Nick shrugged. He hadn't thought of a better plan.

He left the coffee shop, dragging his feet. After scrutinizing the dozens of tired faces in the concourse and looking in vain for an empty seat, he parked his bulk on the tiled floor in front of the "Arrivals and Departures" display. A larger-than-life statue of the previous Advisor, her eyes haughty and oblivious to her surroundings, loomed over the travelers in this area of the station. Nick leaned against the statue so he wouldn't have to look at it.

His gaze flitted around the concourse. If he asked the wrong person, could he be arrested? Thankfully, there was freedom of speech here, as in Canada and everywhere else across the World Federation. And it wasn't like he was advocating for marriage or parenting or any other system of abuse. He was just looking for a facility where such criminal practices occurred. If questioned, he could claim to be a freelance investigator, planning to share any information he obtained with government officials.

Still, he couldn't be sure a police officer wouldn't arrest him, at least take him in for questioning. In any case, if his efforts could end up saving Beatrice's life, that risk was worth taking.

After eating the last of his candy bars, Nick closed his eyes. In his mind, he saw Ruah, writhing and screaming in the flames. And himself, bent over, nauseated, watching the horror unfold, utterly helpless to stop it.

That's it. I'm not going to waste any more time.

To bolster his courage, Nick imagined he was alone in a large auditorium. He took a deep breath and shouted, "I'm looking for the Island House. I'm looking for the Island House. I'm looking for the Island House." He felt like a madman.

He opened his eyes. Dozens of people stared at him, a few shaking their heads.

A middle-aged woman with tangled hair strode over and dropped a pamphlet in his lap. It said, "Attention all mankeys! Cut the excess and join the winning team. Free information session with Dr. Ramses. Sunday, July 8, at 2 p.m. at the Des Moines Renaissance Clinic."

Nick didn't know whether the pamphlet referred to a weight-loss program or a sex reassignment operation, but he didn't care to read further. He scrunched up the pamphlet, shut his eyes again and continued his mantra, though not as loudly. "Looking for the Island House. Looking for the Island House. Looking for the Island House."

"Young man, is that where you want to go?"

Nick looked up to find two women with silver hair and faint smiles leaning over him. Each woman clutched a brown leather-bound book.

"Have you heard of the Island House?" Nick asked.

"Of course," replied the woman with the deeper wrinkles. "People think heaven is like a small island not everyone can fit on. But really, there is room for one and all. As the Good Book says, 'Whosoever shall call upon the name of the Lord shall be saved.' My name's Mary and this is Candice. We'll show you the way to your destination."

Nick wondered whether these slick missionaries actually knew about the Island House. Wasn't

Severed Roots

Christianity rooted in family values? He gathered his courage. "Do you believe in marriage and family?"

"Oh my gosh, that would be bigamy," Mary said. "We're married to God. Besides, it's illegal."

Nick felt stupid. Hadn't Angelina complained that religions changed with the times? Then he told himself he had nothing to lose. "But isn't there anything good about families?"

The two women looked at each other, then frowned at him.

"Young man," Candice replied. "Since the beginning of history, siblings have been antagonistic toward each other. Cain killed his brother, Abel. Jacob hated his brother, Esau. Joseph's brothers wanted to kill him and threw him into a pit. What do you think God has been trying to tell us?"

Nick sighed and waved his hand dismissively. Candice removed a sandwich from her purse and dropped it in Nick's lap. "We'll pray for you," she said, and the two women walked away. Attached to the cellophane wrap was a card with an address and the words "Jesus Loves You."

Nick was grateful for the food but resented the motive.

He devoured the sandwich, not caring what was in it, and sat for an hour, calling out now and then like a lone voice in the wilderness. *Island House, Island*

House, Island House. He kept the volume down—he'd seen the security guard glaring at him a few times.

By now, Nick needed to use a bathroom. Ambling to the facilities marked WOMEN and NONWOMEN, he was taken aback by the sight of a young woman walking toward him. She appeared to be pregnant.

"Uh, excuse me. Do you know where the Island House is?" Nick asked.

The woman stopped and laughed. "I've been asked that question before, especially here at the station. I'm afraid I can't help you. What exactly *is* the Island House?"

Nick glanced around, licking his lips. "It's a place where women can find fertile mankeys and become pregnant."

"Really? How much do they pay? My salary's crappy, considering the discomfort I have to endure." She looked Nick up and down.

"I have no idea how it works," said Nick, self-conscious beneath her scrutiny. "I've never been there. What they do is actually illegal." The words tumbled out before he could think better of it. He tightened his lips. *Why am I always such an ape-brain?*

"I'm not surprised," the woman said. "Must be run by the Hardinians."

Nick hoped the Island House was run by the Progressives rather than the Hardinians. But unless he was sure that was the case, there was no point raising that prospect with this pregnant woman.

He blinked. *I have nothing to lose.* He took a step toward the woman and whispered, "Would you be interested in visiting the Island House with me, if we can locate it?"

"Are you kidding? I could lose my job." She took a decisive step backwards. "Besides, the Hardinians are dangerous."

Nick swallowed, apologized to the woman for having bothered her and turned to the NONWOMEN sign.

"Can I offer you a shower and a place to sleep?"

Nick opened his eyes.

A slender redhead in a tight blouse revealing the crease between her breasts hovered over him. Her hand was on his shoulder. "I've a flat 'round the corner."

Nick's heart pounded. He glanced at his watch: 3:15 a.m. He had dozed off while leaning against the portrait of the Advisor.

The woman's nails dug through the fabric of Nick's shirt, and her fingers clutched his shoulder.

A pervert. "No, thanks. I prefer the hard, dusty floor," Nick said, sardonically.

"Oh. I was hoping you were, y'know..." she leaned over and whispered in his ear, "...a Hardinian." The woman straightened and sauntered off.

Nick closed his eyes, seeking in vain to return to the comfort of sleep. "Ilenhowz, Ilan house, Ilanows," he rattled off, drowsily.

A thought crawled to the front of his sleep-deprived mind. He sat up straight, his arms and neck prickling with raw energy. *Of course! People are afraid to talk. Maybe there's a message on the pamphlet that earlier woman dropped in my lap. Some clue about the location of the Island House.* He scanned his surroundings, trying to remember where he had discarded the scrunched-up pamphlet.

At that moment, a lanky man, sitting on the floor about twenty feet away, called out, "Hey, bud. You lookin' for the Island House?"

Nick scrambled to his feet and hurried over to the man. He had shoulder-length hair, wore a coffee-stained T-shirt and smelled of tobacco. "Do you know about the Island House?"

"'Course. It's a cult. Buddy of mine went there coupla years ago."

Nick blinked. A *cult*? "Why'd he go?"

"Heard he'd get a free place to sleep, so he stole a bike and took off. Never heard from him again."

This was his first real lead. Maybe this guy knew the road his friend had taken.

"Where's it located?"

"Near Cedar Hill, 'bout thirty miles from here."

Nick crouched next to him. "Do you know whereabouts?"

"Yeah, coupla miles east, just past the lake. But..."

"But what?"

"Like I said, they fry your brains."

The man showed him the location on the map on Nick's phone, and Nick hurried to retrieve his bike.

A half hour later, he was pedaling up and down dark, hilly roads, past farmlands dotted with dairy cattle and smelling of manure. The warm, early summer breeze caressed his cheeks.

Soon the road became pitted with potholes, and Nick had to slow down as he wove around them, straining to spot them in the pale light of the night. He also wasn't used to this much fresh air and exercise and found it difficult to keep his focus on the road.

Gradually, the sky brightened, and a few fluffy clouds appeared on the horizon.

The next stretch was uphill. Nick stood on the pedals, his upper body bent over, his neck and back soaked with perspiration. He got himself into a rhythm, uttering "Be-a-trice" under his breath with each downward push of his aching legs.

Nego Huzcotoq

The journey seemed endless. Nick's throat was dry. He felt weak and had to concentrate to keep his balance, but he had no food or drink left. His head throbbed.

The landscape turned darker as ominous grey clouds began to move in. Twenty minutes later, the sky cracked open, and a violent downpour erupted. Nick gritted his teeth as the rain soaked him, but his discomfort only strengthened his determination, and he increased his speed.

The rain ended as abruptly as it had begun, the clouds dispersed, and soon the hot sun dried his face and arms and toasted his clothes. A thin coating of steam rose off the blacktop. Nick stopped pedaling. A cluster of five brownstone buildings sat on a hilltop, surrounded by protective fencing. The view was exquisite: woodlands, hills, valleys and a beautiful serene lake. *This must be it.* Nick's chest swelled as he took in a deep breath of damp, earth-scented air. He peeled off his T-shirt, swung it in a wide circle above his head and hurled a cry of delight.

Nick pedaled toward the centre building.

CHAPTER EIGHTEEN

Nick neared the hilltop, and squinted at a faded lawn sign:

WARNING:
AUTHORIZED PERSONNEL
AND VISITORS ONLY
TRESPASSERS WILL BE PROSECUTED

He hesitated, shrugged and then continued biking up the grade. The gravel crunched under the tires, and the sun warmed his shoulders. He reached the fence, which was topped with razor wire. Above the razor wire, an ornate sign announced:

ESMERALDA PENITENTIARY

Nick froze. *A prison?* Had he made a mistake and gone in the wrong direction? He couldn't have. He'd been careful about following the map.

What if the lanky man at the train station had played a trick on him? When people sought directions, did the scumbag get his kicks by fooling them? Or maybe he was content to receive coffee or cigarettes in return for his "helpfulness."

Ape-brain! Nick slammed his open hand on the bar of his bike. *I've been duped. What do I do now?* He was weak, hungry, and worst of all, dangerously thirsty. Pedaling back to the station in the heat of day was out of the question.

Nick stepped off his bike, lowered it onto the grass and dropped to his knees. He pressed his blistered palms against the cool ground. He thought of waiting there in his sweat-stiffened clothes until some guard spotted him and, out of mercy, took him to the prison hospital.

This time, Karla wouldn't visit and comfort him. *God, why did I lie to Karla? Why did I spy on her boss? What kind of friend am I?*

A wave of nausea engulfed him. What if someone had found the microcamera in Dr. Stone's office by now? He could be a wanted mankey on the run. They might have already broadcast his description everywhere, including this prison. He wiped his brow and shook his head. No, they wouldn't alert authorities this far away...would they?

He thought of Beatrice and for a moment felt good about himself. At least he'd done all this for her, to make her happy. Should he call her to let her know that? No, Morrie had warned him not to contact her.

Wait a minute. Maybe Morrie knows where the Island House is. Maybe I'm close to the place and he could guide me. Maybe it's time I trusted that oddball. I've nothing to lose.

Crouching on a patch of brittle, yellow grass between two small thorn bushes, Nick reached for his phone.

As he keyed Morrie's number, an astute thought formed in his mind: *Better that Morrie doesn't know that I'm likely wanted by the police. He could think I'm interested in the Island House more as a physical refuge than for ideological reasons. He might be less willing to help me.*

Seconds later, Morrie's face appeared on the screen. His image wavered in and out, but his voice was strong, and he sounded surprised, even excited, as he greeted Nick. Morrie said, "You look like you've been in a war zone." Nick grinned. The image flickered and died, but soon came back. Nick licked his chapped lips. *Might be signal jamming from the prison.*

Nick poured out everything—his work for Karla, his clandestine search through the government's network (prudently leaving out the detail about his failure to retrieve the microcamera) and arriving at this prison. Even with the bad reception, Morrie's face pinched with concern as he told him about Beatrice's suicide plan and his desire to help her.

"When's her birthday?"

"In August. I don't know the exact date."

"Why didn't you ask her?"

Nick felt a lump in his throat and swallowed. "A friend knows when your birthday is. If I asked when her birthday was, she'd think I wasn't really her friend."

There was a long pause. Then Morrie said, "Okay, my friend. Let's deal with your physical dehydration now, and we'll deal with your mental dehydration another time. Here's what I want you to do…"

Light from the blistering sun sparkled off the high walls of razor-ribbon wire and fencing. Nick was on a one-way path past barbed wire, armed-guard towers, motion sensors and guard dogs. He could no longer turn back. Through a sequence of remote-control actions that made him wish time would move faster, officers finally enabled him to pass through the double electric fence leading to the visitors' entrance.

Before him was a three-story brown building, the bricks faded with age.

Severed Roots

The front tire of his bike squeaked as he walked it over to a darkened security window.

"Where are you going?" said an icy voice that jostled his nerves.

"I've been sent by Canada's Department of Mental Health to investigate—"

"Place your ID inside the tray and take two steps back."

Nick couldn't see the person behind the window. He imagined his every gesture and word was scrutinized and recorded.

Having surrendered his Canadian Government ID card, Nick was given a form. Following Morrie's instructions, under "Purpose of Visit," he wrote, "To study whether entertainment might help improve the mental health of the prisoners, in particular, having inmates put on magic shows for each other." As directed, Nick slid the completed form along with his phone into the slot below the security window.

He had just secured his bike on the nearby rack when a female guard appeared from a side door. She wore blue coveralls, cinched lightly at the waist with a khaki belt. Dull eyes peered at him from beneath her garrison cap as she pivoted and escorted Nick past an open courtyard. With a tour guide's cadence, she rattled off information about the prison features as they passed.

Nick looked dutifully at everything the guard pointed out. He listened to her describe the dimensions of the exercise yard and paid close attention as she identified a separate wing labeled "Mental Health Unit." His mind wandered as he tuned out her description of the meals prepared in the kitchen, and he marveled at the size of the pots and pans dangling from hooks on the wall. He wanted to ask if there was a faucet or water fountain he could drink from, but she was talking nonstop, and he couldn't decide when and how to interrupt.

They descended two sets of winding, dusty stairs. Nick's heart beat faster. Where was she taking him? The air was cooler, and the swishing of electric sliding doors controlled by officers in glass-enclosed stations greeted them at every turn along the dark, concrete walls.

What was he doing in a place like this?

All for Beatrice.

They approached the west wing, which, the guard said, housed the cell blocks. The sound of banging doors and mankeys yelling and swearing echoed down the austere, discoloured halls. An electrical mechanism clicked, unlocking a metal door. As the guard pulled the heavy door open, Nick gagged at the stench of urine and sweat. Before him was a cell, eight-by-ten feet, made of reinforced cement—bare walls and a ceiling, with no window. The only furniture was a bed—a steel frame topped by a thin mattress—and a table. A steel toilet and sink occupied a corner of the cell.

"A visitor from Canada's Ministry of Tomorrow," the female guard bellowed in a deep voice.

A prisoner with a huge muscular body, displaying an array of intricate tattoos on both forearms, jumped up from his cot and swore in a loud voice, saying he was not in the mood to entertain guests.

Nick gasped and tried to move away, but the guard blocked his path and nudged him into the cell. She tersely informed the prisoner he had no choice—he *would* speak to the visitor. The metal door slammed shut, and the lock reengaged with a click.

The inmate took a few steps toward Nick, looking him up and down, getting so close Nick inhaled his putrid breath. He glared at Nick for a long time. The muscles in Nick's neck tightened.

"I-I don't know why they brought me to you," Nick said, taking a step back. "I just came here to get a general tour of the place." His heart pounded.

"Why? You considering movin' in? Checking out the *Holiday Inn*?" His voice was deep and reverberated throughout the tiny cell.

"No. I—I mean, they sent me—"

"I'll tell you why they brought you to me. 'Cause I'm the friggin house historian. Been here since before you learned to brush your teeth. Know this place like the numbers on the back of my hand. What department are you with?"

"Mental Health."

"Another one!" His eyebrows shot up, and his head swayed with incredulity. "In the last three months, we've had half a dozen of you airheads here. Mind you, all of them women. They wanted to understand why we have so many mental cases and what we do about it. Problem is, they never stay long enough to find out the answer."

"What do you mean?" Nick asked.

"What do I *mean*?" His large jaw muscle twitched. "You try living in this madhouse twenty-four hours a day, seven days a week. When you live among crazies, you go crazy. In this cell block there's an average of one stabbing a week." He grasped Nick's hand and squeezed it so hard Nick squirmed. "Name's Dunn."

"Nick. Nick Wong."

"So you must be one of them graduates from the Children's Centres. Shortchanged you with a Chinese name to help you forget who you were. I'll tell you, none of us here know who we are. We only know what we used to be—robbers, rapists, arsonists, cop killers, you name it."

Nick needed to focus on his mission: to find the Island House. But how could he achieve that? Other than helping him gain access to this prison and arming him with a code phrase to use as a last resort, Morrie had left Nick to his own devices.

Should he ask Dunn if he'd be interested in Nick helping him organize a magic show? The surly prisoner would laugh in his face. Although… maybe if Nick lied and said he was an escape artist…?!

Dunn walked past Nick to the narrow iron-meshed slot in the door. "Listen, you came at a bad time. Rec's in one minute. Guard! Visitor wants to talk to you."

A minute later, Nick found himself outside the cell in the company of a tall, flat-chested woman with a strong jaw and several missing teeth. She identified herself as Betty.

A loud buzz went off, then a spray of clicking sounds. Inmates filed out of their cells. Nick stood with Betty in the narrow corridor between two rows of open metal doors. His airway constricted and his body tensed as the inmates brushed past him on both sides, some pausing long enough to glare their suspicions.

When the hallway cleared, Betty escorted Nick down a dimly lit metallic inclined platform. They entered a wide area with a small exercise station. The space filled with the sound of cursing. Around Nick, inmates pumped weights, trying to outdo one another. Others stood by the pool tables, focused on their games.

Betty's hands dangled from her pockets. "There's Ryder over there, bending over the pool table." She gestured with a jerk of her chin. "He's the official jailhouse prostitute but isn't very active. Racked with too many infections."

Nick squirmed.

"This unit houses sex offenders," Betty continued. "The thieves are in a different unit, together with the dope traffickers and the cop killers."

Nick stared at the inmates while trying to absorb her words. "Are there Hardinians here?"

"In a special unit, two floors up. They're growing like weeds. Sentenced for inciting violence. One's on death row for setting up medical experiments to try to reinstate mankeys' sex drive. What exactly are you here to investigate?"

Nick turned and looked into Betty's rough face. "The mental health of the prisoners."

"You came to the right place." Betty flashed a checkerboard grin, revealing gaps in her teeth. "Mental health problems are rampant in Esmeralda. Especially among the female population."

Nick raised his eyebrows. "There are female prisoners here too?"

Betty nodded. "In a different part of the building. Most of 'em are real nutcases—convicted for abducting babies from Children's Centres and attempting to raise them on their own. A few are mankey lovers."

Severed Roots

Nick was grateful for the clanging noises of weight plates, inmates arguing over the leg curl machine, yelled profanities. Thankfully, nobody seemed to be paying much attention to him or Betty.

"Here in this section, we have the pedophiles, the masochists, the sadists, the voyeurs—you name it." She counted on her fingers as she listed the categories. "We force them into chemical castration, of course. If we can't completely suppress the deviant urges that way, we do behavioural modification too."

Nick nodded, hoping to appear knowledgeable.

"Anyway, you can't really blame these people. I might have been one of them if I hadn't decided to change."

Nick looked at her.

"Listen, Mr..."

"Call me Nick."

"Nick, I used to be a 230-pound balding guy, with a fuse so short it cost me my front teeth and many a black eye. One day, as I lay on the street, plastered, a driver—must have felt disgusted by the sight of me—headed straight in my direction and missed me by this much." Betty held out her index finger and thumb an inch apart.

"I realized then that it was only a matter of time before I ended up six feet under," she continued. "So, I had an epiphany and decided to go under the knife. I tell you, since I woke up in the clinic with a new body, I feel like I've joined the winning team."

Nick widened his eyes. "Are there other guards who made the switch?"

Betty shrugged. "I'd say 'bout a third of us are former mankeys. In some prisons it's as high as 70 percent. The job's a good fit. Having been mankeys ourselves, we can relate to the prisoners."

Nick looked away from Betty. *There's so much I can learn here, but am I getting any closer to finding this secret place where families are raised?* A loud buzz sounded over the intercom.

"Rec's over," said Betty. "I'll take you back to the historian."

Nick and Betty made their way back down the hall to the cell block. She ushered him into Dunn's cell.

"Had a pleasant tour?" Dunn asked, after the door clicked shut. "You should know, the staff lie about what really goes on in here. Especially the warden. She creates a façade that we're all dangerous and violent. They give us extra canteen money for bodybuilding and to go to the tattoo parlour so we look tougher in the media. The government loves that. If we don't comply—if we don't yell and curse and fight—the staff will instigate brawls. They also force us to take programs but fix them so most of us fail. They don't want us re'bilitated."

"Why not?"

"Why *not*? Don't you have half a brain?" Dunn snorted. "We're museum pieces. Mankeys from the Age of Oppression. They bring kids here on tours so they won't question the New World Order when they grow up.

Nick's head was spinning. When he lived in the Children's Centre, they were never taken on a trip to a prison. Maybe this was a recent initiative or done only in the US. In any case, if what Dunn said was true, the US government was deceiving and brainwashing the masses. *Holy smokes.* A bit like *Twenty Eighty-Four*, that novel everyone had to plough through in grade ten, warning against totalitarianism.

Nick shuddered at the thought, then pushed it aside. He needed to double down on his mission.

"What are you in for?"

"Spousal rape—a month before they outlawed marriage. I got life. Only problem is, I was framed."

"What happened?"

"One morning, in a rush to leave for work, I kissed my spouse without having obtained her prior written consent. We froze and looked at each other, realizing what I had done, then broke into a laugh. We decided then and there to forgo filling out that ridiculous legal form each morning. Well, one day, she used that against me." Dunn's face sagged, and he shook his head slowly.

"To this day, I don't know if she was trying to trick me... That's what really hurts."

Nick studied Dunn's face, trying to picture him as an innocent man.

"Look, there are bad apples here, but I reckon half the guys are innocent. It's the same everywhere. Frankly, they don't know what to do with us. Right now, about a quarter of births are non-girls, and I hear the Advisor wants to reduce it to one in ten. I reckon one day—unless there's a bloody revolution—we'll be phased out altogether on the planet. Except, of course, for the lucky few of us they'll still need as donors."

Nick recalled Morrie's instructions. He took a deep breath. "I wonder what *Mrs. Fullerfaith* would say about that."

Dunn froze. He fixed his gaze on Nick. He took a step forward, and his eyes darted in several directions before returning to Nick. Dunn moved his face close to Nick's.

"*You know Mrs. F?*" he whispered.

Nick's heart pounded. "I—a friend of mine told me it's a code. If I dropped the name it would signal to you that I'm..."

"That you're *what*?" Dunn glared at him.

"I-I want to help you get out." A panic reaction. A lie. Nick wished Morrie's instructions had been more detailed.

Severed Roots

"How? What do you know about Mrs. Fullerfaith? Have you ever been *there*?"

Nick didn't know where *there* was. He needed to choose his words carefully.

"Listen, I need to be going. I hope to be back soon, though, and we'll talk some more." Nick approached the door and leaned toward the narrow aperture. "Guard! I'm ready to leave."

At that moment, Nick felt the powerful blow of Dunn crashing against him, taking them both to the floor. He grabbed Nick's left arm and bent it against his back. Nick yelped in pain.

"If this was a setup"—Dunn twisted Nick's arm more—"I swear, I will kill you."

Click. The door unlocked, and a guard jumped in and pointed a baton at Dunn. "Release him instantly, or face the hole for a week."

Dunn loosened his grip, helped Nick up, dusted him off and said with a wink, "Come back tomorrow, and we'll continue our wrestling lesson."

On his way out, Nick spotted a water fountain. He bent and drank from it as though he had a camel's reservoir to fill. Patting drops from his chapped lips, he straightened himself and vowed never to set foot in a prison again.

Then he shuddered. *Where shall I go?*

CHAPTER NINETEEN

Dazed, **Karla slid** a chair up to Doreeta Stone's desk.

Her lover's eyes blazed. "I knew I shouldn't have agreed to it!"

Karla rolled the microcamera between her thumb and index finger. "I'm stunned too. Nick was the epitome of honesty and integrity."

"The epitome of honesty and integrity?" Doreeta stood and paced back and forth. "We should have known. We can never trust mankeys." Her gaze flitted around the room. "We have to assess the extent of the security breach. I want you in charge of that."

Karla took a slow, deep breath, drumming her fingers on Doreeta's desk. "It's been four days since he was here. He hasn't returned my calls. We have to find him."

"*Find*, my dear, is not the right word. We will hunt him down. Mercilessly."

Karla's fingers turned cold. "What do you want me to do?" She tried to maintain an even voice.

Doreeta sniffed the air in disdain. "Hunting him down? That'll be my job."

Karla staggered back to her office, her head spinning. *My own brother! Doreeta could do something rash. Should I try to warn Nick? Or should my loyalty be to her?*

Karla hated herself for these conflicted feelings. Ambivalence was mankeyish.

Nick braked, slid off his bike and slouched onto the ground. He was about a quarter mile from the prison grounds, far beyond the electric fence. He felt if he closed his eyes he might drift away and never wake up.

He pulled out his phone.

"He did *what*?" Morrie's curly reddish beard took up most of the video screen. The image was sharper and more stable than the last time.

Nick repeated what he had said, finishing with "I felt like my arm was going to snap."

"Why, that's wonderful."

"What?"

"He obviously knows about the Island House, maybe even where it's located. You need to go see him again and earn his trust."

Nick rubbed the back of his elbow. *See him again? Are you nuts?* But he couldn't think of a viable alternative. He didn't want to abandon his mission, and Morrie was knowledgeable and willing to help him.

"How do I do that?"

Morrie pulled his chin in. "You're asking the wrong fellow, Mister," he said in a flat voice. "Heck, after your behavior at my house and refusal to open your door for me the next morning, I'm not even sure *I* can trust you."

Nick felt a heaviness in his limbs. *If Morrie no longer wants to help me, who can I turn to?*

Morrie sucked in a long, deep breath. "Look, I already helped you get inside the prison, and I gave you a code word, which you made poor use of. I'm still willing to lend a hand. But you'll need to figure out the next step on your own. I'm rooting for you." He hung up.

"Wait—"

What's with this oddball? He seems to want to test my resolve, but why?

Nick dropped his head to his knees, letting his phone fall in the dirt. His eyelids drooped. A moment later, Beatrice appeared in his imagination with the saddest expression he'd ever seen. She was seated on a bench. Her pained voice rang through his mind. *"Why can't a woman have a baby of her own? Why must it be a crime? Weren't women given wombs?"* Then Beatrice transformed into Karla, and she spoke compassionately but pedagogically. *"Even if something is natural, Nick, it doesn't mean it's right. Our purpose in this world is to transcend our nature, not to surrender to it."*

Nick imagined himself in an abyss, struggling to climb out, seeking an elevation from which he could see all the trees and all the terrain and all the people, a privileged spot where the disparate fragments of his world would come together into something whole and clear.

This mission is about more than making Beatrice happy.

He lifted his head, stood and made his way back to the prison.

"You again?" The voice behind the opaque window at the visitors' entrance was colder than liquid nitrogen. Nick spoke woodenly, his brain numb, explaining he had some unfinished work inside.

As Nick entered Dunn's cell, the prisoner jumped up from his cot as if it were on fire. The female guard—a different one this time—locked the heavy door, leaving them alone.

Nick squared his shoulders, bracing himself for another attack. The contours of the cell came into sharp focus. Strangely, he was not nervous. "I'd like to learn more wrestling moves," Nick joked, hoping to ease the tension.

Dunn stared at him unsmilingly. "You've either lost your mind," he began, "or you've something important to tell me. And it damn well better be important, 'cause in thirty seconds I'm gonna start snapping every bone in your body like they're twigs." He jerked his chin at Nick, motioning him toward the cot.

Nick stood where he was. "Mr. Dunn, I wasn't sent by any ministry. I lied to get in here because I need to find out something."

Dunn's hand flew to his chest. "Well, well, well. Now that I know you're a *liar*, why should I believe anything else you tell me? And don't ever call me 'mister.' I shed my honorific when I turned eight."

"I won't tell you anything. I'll *ask* you. Do you know where the Island House is?"

"The *what*?"

"An underground place where people raise families."

Dunn sat down on the cot and leaned against the wall. After a moment he whispered, "How do I know you're not really with the government? Prove to me you're not."

"You can get the front desk to call the Canadian Ministry of Tomorrow," Nick said. "They'll confirm they never sent me." *Ape-brain. If Dunn did that, the Ministry would know my whereabouts.*

Severed Roots

"Ha! Do you take me for a fool? If it's a setup, of course the government will deny sending you!"

"Look, Mr. Dunn—"

"If you call me 'mister' one more time, I swear I'll rip your tongue out with my bare hands."

"Sorry, Dunn." Nick looked at the floor and licked his lips. He forced himself to speak, although the words came louder and faster than he intended. "I infiltrated the Canadian government's network in order to find out about the Island House, then scraped together almost all my money to buy a train ticket to Des Moines."

Nick raised his head and looked Dunn in the eye. "I slept on the floor in the train station, and then biked five hours straight to get here after some homeless man pointed me in this direction. I'm very tired and very hungry. I—"

"Why should I give a damn about what you want?" Dunn batted his hand. "Spare me the sob story."

Nick's cheeks burned, and he struggled to control the frustration which bubbled inside him. "Okay, Dunn. This woman I know is planning to kill herself if she can't have children. You could be saving a life." He exhaled loudly as a tremor passed through him.

Dunn shrugged. "Like I said, assuming I *am* able to help you, what's in it for me? Why should I care about anybody else?"

Nego Huzcotoq

Nick stood, barely breathing. He considered Dunn's question. He had no answer. Tears he had fought back now rolled down his cheeks.

"I guess you shouldn't," Nick admitted. "I guess we're all just selfish individuals." He wrapped a hand around one of the cell bars to steady himself and wiped his face with the other. "We're each free to live for ourselves, by ourselves." He dropped his hand to his side and faced Dunn squarely. "And when we're on our deathbeds, we'll realize it didn't matter what we did, even for ourselves. It will all be meaningless." Nick spun around. "Guard! I'm ready to leave."

"Thank you for enriching me with your wisdom," Dunn said. As Nick was escorted away, the prisoner let out a shrill laugh that reverberated down the cell block.

Nick picked up his pace, staring down at the guard's heels, relieved to be out of Dunn's presence.

When he reached the narrow exit door, the guard disappeared. Nick's repeated requests to be let out went unanswered. The door remained locked.

A chill ran through Nick's bones. Something wasn't right.

Severed Roots

After what seemed a long time, a robust woman in a guard's uniform appeared and informed him Fred Dunn wished to see him again.

The last thing Nick wanted was to go back into a confined space with that man.

When Nick returned to Dunn's cell, he was surprised to find that a chair and small table had been placed there. On the table were two plates of food and two drinks. Dunn, sitting on his bed in front of the table, motioned for Nick to take the chair.

Dunn's demeanour had completely changed. His eyes were calm, his body relaxed. "Why—" Nick began.

"Now we eat. Later we talk."

Nick frowned. *Is this guy genuine? He must have clout to be able to order fancy meals for two. On the other hand, maybe he's a prankster, who earned special privileges for...what?*

Nick sat down guardedly, expecting Dunn to do something explosive at any moment. Mental disorders were rampant in prisons, he reminded himself.

Regardless, he was starving. The food's delectable aroma filled his nostrils and grabbed at the pit of his stomach. Nick dug into the hot meal of boiled carrots, fried onions, quinoa. and mock turkey. With each swallow, he felt stronger. Within a few minutes, he'd cleaned his plate, while Dunn had barely eaten a third of his meal.

"Oh, my," Dunn said with a wink. "I'd forgotten my esteemed guest was famished. Please accept my apologies for not feeding you sooner. Shall I order some more?"

Nick studied Dunn's face—the slanted forehead, the puffy, dimpled cheeks, the protruding jaw. His features hadn't changed, yet he felt like he was meeting this man for the first time. Maybe Dunn had a split personality.

"I'm fine. Thanks," Nick said.

Dunn leaned back. "So now, my Canadian friend, we talk business."

Dunn put down his fork, picked up a cloth napkin and took his time wiping his mouth. "Yes, I do know where the Island House is. There are six other people in this prison who also know, including the warden, the head of security and Betty, who you met earlier. I'm the only inmate who's in the know. In fact, I'm not really an inmate—I only pretend to be one. That's my full-time job."

Dunn paused. Nick's pulse quickened, but he kept his eyes averted, pretending nonchalance, wary of setting Dunn off again.

"In the twenty or so minutes you were detained, I consulted with these three individuals and persuaded them you're a reasonable risk. I got the green light to tell you where the Island House is located."

Nick's eyebrows shot up.

"Oh, and the warden mentioned she'd received a message from our recruiting officer in Canada. Apparently he had some good words to say about you."

Recruiting officer? Morrie? If Morrie knew all along where the Island House was located, why didn't he share the information with me?

"You have to understand something. Once you enter the Island House, you can't leave."

Nick jerked his head upright and looked directly into Dunn's eyes. "Why?" He recalled the warning the guy in the train station had given: *It's a cult.*

"Top secret facility. We don't want anyone spilling the beans."

"Can you tell me a little about the place? What its—"

Dunn shook his head. "Top-secret facility."

"Okay. Give me a few moments," said Nick.

Dunn nodded.

Nick slouched in his chair, closing his eyes. Should he accept a one-way ticket to the unknown?

He went through a mental list of the important people in his life, trying to figure out whom he would miss. Angelina? A tremor passed through him as he realized he never visited her in the hospital, even though he'd told her he would. Karla? She cared about him, but now that he'd betrayed her, their relationship was likely over. His buddies at the Mankey Bar? Not really—they were an audience for his magic tricks and a distraction from his loneliness. Morrie? Nick was grateful for all his help, and he could still learn from him, but if Morrie was a recruiting officer, he might be allowed to visit Nick. And perhaps there'd be other good mentors at the Island House.

Nick's stomach fluttered. He'd miss Beatrice. She was the reason he'd made the trip here.

Should he ask Dunn if he could return to Ottawa and get Beatrice? It was unlikely the prison officials would let him—he knew too much. And even if they would, it didn't seem right for Nick to try to convince someone to permanently move into a place he himself hadn't yet experienced. All the more so given the Island House was illegal.

He sucked in a quick breath. No—this wasn't just about Beatrice. Something about the world Nick inhabited didn't feel right, and he needed to discover the truth—about family, about society, about human nature. As for Beatrice, he'd figure out a plan later.

Nick shifted in his seat. There was something else. Nick could never again live in Ottawa—or anywhere else in Canada. The microcamera in Dr. Stone's office would certainly be discovered, if it hadn't been already. The police would be in pursuit. He'd be caught, tried and convicted for espionage and thrown in a small, dingy prison cell for who knows how many years. Maybe the Island House was his only refuge.

Nick opened his eyes and sat up straight. "I agree to the condition."

He felt Dunn's penetrating gaze, his searching eyes. It was as if Dunn was still waiting for a reply, as if Dunn had not heard him or perhaps did not believe him.

After an uncomfortably long silence, Dunn slowly nodded. "Good, Nick. I'm confident you understand this is a one-way street. If you're not happy in the Island House, there's no way out. In fact, if someone wanted to leave the Island House and succeeded in escaping—it's never happened—we'd broadcast that person as an offender at large."

Nick furrowed his brow. Dunn leaned back against the wall, clasped his hands behind his head, and stared at Nick for a long time.

"You mean—?"

"It's physically connected to this prison."

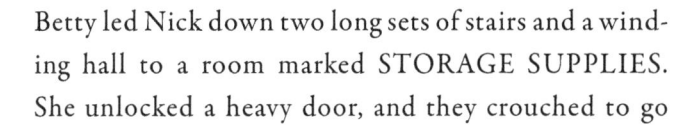

Betty led Nick down two long sets of stairs and a winding hall to a room marked STORAGE SUPPLIES. She unlocked a heavy door, and they crouched to go through the small doorway, stepping into darkness. She switched on a dim light, revealing a dusty empty space a little smaller than Dunn's cell.

Nick's breathing became shallow.

I could still turn back. It's not too late...is it?

Betty made her way to the opposite side of the room and inserted a key in another door. Nick lifted the bottom of his T-shirt to his forehead and pressed it to absorb the sweat. *No, I've reached the point of no return. I now know where the Island House is, so there's no way they'd allow me to go back.*

As she swung the door open, rays of light streamed in through a narrow tunnel a few dozen feet long, lined with some type of reflective material. Nick felt nourished by the sudden light.

"This is it, brother," said Betty. "We call it the birth canal. You're about to start a new life."

Nick squared his shoulders. He gazed at her. For a brief moment he wondered whether her own new life as a woman was as radical as the changes he was about to experience.

"I'll give it my best," he said, waving goodbye. Then he turned to face the future.

CHAPTER TWENTY

Nick blinked rapidly as he left the tunnel and stepped onto a concrete floor. An enormous playground slide in pastel greens, yellows and pinks rose toward an artificial sky. The light from an imitation sun reflected off its wide metallic surface. Two dozen children took turns climbing the tall stairs and, without hesitation, released themselves down the slide and into the outstretched arms of the women or men waiting below. Laughter filled the air. Older adults sat on wooden benches, watching and smiling. A long-legged girl with wavy hair ran past Nick to a grey-bearded man and a bony woman, yelling, "Grandpa, Grandma, did you see how fast I went?"

A strange warmth rose in Nick's chest as fragments of sounds, images and tactile impressions—forgotten for so long—rushed to his consciousness. The squeals of children on a merry-go-round. A freckled boy trying to run up a slippery slide. Boys and girls, arms linked, chanting, "Red rover, red rover, let Nico come over," a grassy field, and little Nick, basking in the attention, sprinting against the wind toward the human chain, mouth open, rain droplets encased in sunshine dampening his face.

Nick tore his eyes away. *I must understand. This unbounded joy is not normal.*

Off to the side stood a pair of large wooden doors. The main entrance to the Island House? Cautiously, he approached. The doors looked strong and heavy, as if fashioned in a different era. Ornate carvings of birds decorated the upper panels. Maybe a hundred years ago someone—probably a man—had spent a week carving out these doors and then smiled to himself when he finished. Nick inhaled their earthy aroma before turning the oversized brass handle to let himself through.

A corridor with pale-blue floor tiles stretched in front of him. He stepped forward. On his left was a door marked "Executive Director."

Nick thought of knocking but didn't want to jar himself from his dream-like state. Slowly turning the handle, he was surprised to find the door unlocked. The room was illuminated by the soft glow of a single light. He paused as his eyes adjusted to the dimness and, strangely, felt the tension leave his body.

Severed Roots

The walls were bare. A middle-aged woman sat behind a dark rosewood desk. The only item on its surface was an old-fashioned intercom. The woman wore a flowery blouse. A heavy necklace weighted by an olive-green gemstone adorned her throat. As Nick approached the crimson-padded chair on the other side of her desk, she looked up.

"Welcome, Nick. We're happy to receive newcomers." The woman smiled, displaying a set of milk-white teeth, and gestured for him to be seated.

Nick lowered himself onto the chair. "What's the purpose of this place?"

The woman leaned forward. Her charcoal eyes searched his face. "You came to an underground facility, a place from which you cannot leave, and don't know its purpose?"

Nick swallowed. His armpits grew hot.

The executive director pulled her sharply angled manicured eyebrows down. "I don't know a lot about you, Nick, but I know why you're here—like all our residents, you're drawn to something more meaningful than what is offered outside these walls." She tilted her head slightly. "My job is to help create a new society, to help build a community for the future, and there is no better—no healthier—way to ensure a brighter tomorrow than by nurturing happy children—something not possible in the world at large. Not at the present time."

"I see. Are you affiliated with the Hardinians?"

"God forbid, no. We call ourselves the Progressives. The Hardinians seek a return to male dominance and female subjugation, and as I'm sure you know, they're planning a bloody revolution to try to achieve that. By contrast, we believe in dignity for all and in the power of education."

Amazing. Nick felt vindicated in his efforts to find the Island House. Morrie would be proud of him. "I want to help."

"What skills do you offer?"

"I'm a magician."

She clapped both hands together. "Excellent! Then you can entertain the children. Magic will stimulate their minds, their curiosity. I will have our Volunteer Coordinator get in touch with you once you've settled into our residences. In the meantime, Ahmed will show you around our facilities."

She spoke into the intercom. A moment later, a slender, balding gentleman appeared. He leaned on a walking stick.

"I will be happy to show our valued newcomer around, Mrs. Fullerfaith," he said, in a Middle Eastern accent. He turned to Nick. "First, I will take you to your quarters."

"No," said Nick. "Please, I prefer to see this place now."

Severed Roots

Ahmed glanced at Mrs. Fullerfaith, then shrugged. "As you wish, sir."

His guide proceeded to the corridor, and Nick followed, squinting as he adjusted to the brighter light.

As Ahmed rattled off the statistics, Nick learned there were 805 permanent residents in the underground facility. They lived in their own homes, which were nestled in semidetached blocks. Ahmed smiled gently, nodding at Nick. "You will feel at home here. Approximately 40 percent of our people are single, sir. The balance are married, and many have been blessed with children."

"How is this...community supported?" Nick inquired.

"It's maintained through a covert international network of private donors and volunteer workers. Some of the workers are former Esmeralda inmates."

Ahmed explained that many residents were schooled for half the day and did community work during the other half, such as preparing meals, cleaning communal buildings and maintaining the gardens, which were all underground. A few had administrative jobs.

"We have a gym, library and play school for the youngsters," said Ahmed. He placed a hand on Nick's shoulder. "We have a large health clinic—where, in addition to addressing normal health problems, our doctors help to restore men's libido and fertility."

Nick took a step backward, pretending to look at something on the floor, and Ahmed's hand fell back to his side. Undeterred, he continued his lecture. "They perform what on the outside are considered illegal medical procedures on men, as well as on women who took mandatory government-issued drugs to relieve their MS symptoms.

"Our success rate on men is about 50 percent, and we are constantly improving," Ahmed said, his eyes twinkling. "For the women, it is almost 100 percent."

Beatrice. Although she'd been trashing her meds anyway.

They reached the end of a hallway. "The School of Life," Ahmed said, pointing down the staircase with his walking stick, "is our crowning achievement. It is in large part what keeps the residents from wanting to leave."

Nick widened his eyes. A *school...of life?*

"The teachers have undergone rigorous screening and were hand-selected for their character as well as their ability to teach. They are of the highest calibre. It is their calling. They are not paid."

Nick raised an eyebrow.

"Every one of our full-time teachers has a family on site. They have everything they need here." Ahmed turned to Nick and peered deep into his eyes. "This is a place where people genuinely care about each other." His voice quivered. "A place where we laugh together and cry together."

Nick remained silent. He recalled his years in the Children's Centre, where he would cry alone.

Ahmed led Nick down a winding set of stairs to a lower floor. "The atmosphere here is electric. People are growing and changing. It is an inspiration and wonder to behold."

"Uh, people change...into what?" Nick asked, feeling his pulse speed up.

Laughter lines appeared at the corners of Ahmed's eyes. "The goal of the school is to rediscover the age-old values and practical wisdom that have kept humanity going since the dawn of civilization, despite its numerous setbacks. We foster an atmosphere of open inquiry and mutual respect."

Ahmed turned to Nick and winked. "Questions are highly encouraged."

Nick smiled and nodded.

Leaning on his walking stick, Ahmed motioned in the direction of the classrooms that lined both sides of the long corridor. "I will now leave you. Feel free to drop in on any of our classes, even if they are in progress, to get an idea of what you might be interested in exploring further. I will meet back with you later to show you to your room."

Nick thanked his guide, who bowed and left. With a lightness in his chest, he walked the corridor. He stopped at the first door—pink and blue, with the sign "Gender Roles" next to it.

He opened the door cautiously and found himself in the back of a lecture hall. A slim brunette in the last row turned toward him, jumped up and gestured for him to take her seat, which he hesitantly did. The woman stepped nimbly through the audience and soon found another seat for herself.

Nick turned his attention to the speaker, an animated young man in a green suit, with a round face and a full black beard. He didn't have the Rite of Passage tattoo on the back of his hands.

"The belief that, except for physiological differences, women are the same as men discouraged women from recognizing their distinctive strengths and pursuing their unique contribution to society. The struggle for equality last century, rooted in a justifiable—I repeat, a justifiable—desire for greater respect by men, was distorted into a struggle for sameness."

Morrie or Hanna could be giving the same speech, Nick realized with a jolt.

"Men and women have different roles in society, but gender roles need not be constricting. Think of a workplace. Role specialization empowers an organization to reach its goals more efficiently, while providing its workers with a more palpable sense of contribution and greater job satisfaction."

The speaker went on to explain that there are two types of energies in the world—yin and yang—each containing a little bit of the other. Yin is associated with the female qualities of *being* and *harmony*. Yang is associated with the male drive to "conquer" or change the world. He said that, while generally speaking, women are naturally more spiritual and represent humanity's higher ideal, men have a crucial role in the betterment of the world, but they must work on themselves extra hard to avoid falling into depravity.

The ideas intrigued Nick, and he wanted to hear more. But he was also eager to find out what other classes were available. Time was of the essence; he needed to learn as much as he could about the Island House so he could decide whether or not to try to get Beatrice, somehow, to join this community. Spotting an elderly man heading toward the door, he seized the opportunity and slipped out after him.

Nick proceeded down the brightly lit corridor and stopped at the next set of double doors. He studied the words on the whiteboard: "INTRODUCTION TO DATING AND MATING."

Wow. Were these activities alive and well in this strange world? He felt he'd stumbled into some kind of time warp and been thrown decades into the past.

Nego Huzcotoq

He let himself into the room.

"In truth, you can never find Mr. Right." The female lecturer punched the air, emphasizing the word *find*. "The best you can do is establish an acceptable degree of compatibility with your date and decide whether you want to commit to a lifelong, loving relationship with him, thereby *rendering* him Mr. Right. Any other questions?"

A dozen hands flew up. A woman with short curly hair and a long slender neck asked, "Should I make myself sexually enticing when I date?"

"Good question," said the lecturer. "A woman who exposes her body in order to win admirers often finds men want her for her body and not necessarily for who she is inside. Is that your goal? I wouldn't recommend it. Now, if you cover yourself up, there's less chance a man will fall in love with the outer curvature of your flesh as opposed to the inner quality of your personality."

"Which is what I'd prefer," the curly-haired woman said. "So...I guess I'm responsible for how men look at me."

"Not so fast," said the lecturer, raising her voice a notch. "Men's sexual issues are ultimately their responsibility. They need to learn to regulate their thoughts and impulses. But if you can help men view you the way you want to be viewed, isn't it in your best interest to do so?"

Severed Roots

Nick had difficulty relating to the speaker's words, while many in the audience nodded their heads in agreement.

"Of course," added the lecturer, "here in the Island House there are only about three hundred singles, and everyone pretty much knows every one else. So dating is a whole different ball game. But remember, I'm also preparing you for life outside these walls if and when that becomes possible."

"Is it good to have premarital relations?" asked a dainty redhead, who looked to be in her early twenties.

"It depends on what you mean by 'good,'" said the lecturer. "It's certainly highly pleasurable."

A few people in the audience laughed.

"Any downside?" persisted the redhead.

The lecturer smiled. She spoke clearly and unhurriedly, as if wanting to make sure every word was understood. "You have to understand something. Touch is a powerful force. It can create an illusion of emotional intimacy and a feeling of commitment that may have little basis in reality. This prevents an objective assessment of the other person's character and the suitability of a permanent relationsh—"

"Vat about suitability *in bed*?" a deep Russian-accented voice called out.

The lecturer located the man quickly and locked eyes with him. "Thank you for that excellent question,

Dmitri. What do you think? In the past, countless couples got married after blissful experiences in bed, only to discover they had vastly different opinions on how to deal with each other's parents or what type of house to buy or how to raise their children."

Dmitri shifted in his seat, then crossed his arms over his chest. "Well, why does life have to be so damn complicated? Why all zis rules? Why can't we just live our lives ze way we feel?"

The lecturer narrowed her eyes at him. "No one should tell you how to live, Dmitri. You're free to choose your behaviours. Unfortunately, though, you have to live with the natural consequences."

Dmitri sat frozen for a few seconds, as if in a trance. Then, slowly, he got up. He brought his hands together in prayer-like fashion, raised them to rest on top of his head and bent his upper body ninety degrees toward the lecturer in a dramatic, deep bow. He straightened himself, turned and ambled to the exit.

A chill ran through Nick. *What's with that guy?* The sensation, however, subsided as he sat through the rest of the questions, enraptured. He felt like he was in second grade again, learning to add and subtract.

CHAPTER TWENTY-ONE

Ahmed assigned Nick a room in the residential quarters. The room felt smaller than his apartment in Ottawa but was clean and uncluttered. There was no kitchen or bathroom—the toilets and showers were down the hall and shared communally.

Over the next few weeks, Nick attended as many classes as he could. He also spent four hours a day helping with miscellaneous chores as well as entertaining children with magic tricks—improvising, because he didn't have his equipment.

He'd go to bed exhausted and wake up hungry for the day ahead. Oddly, even though no natural sunshine reached any part of the underground facility, it felt like the Island House was bathed in light. For the first time, Nick thought seriously about dating, marriage and being a father—things he'd never imagined were still possible. He even dropped into the health clinic for a physical examination, including an assessment of the effects of the Rite of Passage injection on his sex drive. The doctor prescribed pills to help counter the effects.

At times, he thought of Beatrice, especially while lying in bed at night before sleep overtook him. Her threat of self-immolation had inspired his journey. *Truth is a friend that never betrays,* she was fond of saying. He may have found the wellspring of truth here in the Island House, but she was still yearning to live that truth. She should be here with him.

But other times, he thought differently. It had been only a few weeks since he'd arrived here on June 30. There was still so much he didn't understand about the peculiar ideology of this clandestine community; it was so different from everything he'd ever been exposed to. The fact that Beatrice suffered from MS and had declared, after a traumatic experience at the mall, that she would commit suicide didn't give Nick the moral authority to decide where she was to spend the rest of her life.

One morning, while Nick was mopping the halls, Mrs. Fullerfaith approached him, her eyebrows drawn together.

"I've been hearing good things about you, Nick. The children love your magic tricks, and the staff in the School of Life have commented on your insatiable curiosity and eagerness to learn. Everyone I talk to thinks you're adjusting well."

"I belong here," Nick replied.

Mrs. Fullerfaith smiled. "Come with me to my office."

Five minutes later, Nick was again seated in the crimson-padded chair he sat in the first day he met Mrs. Fullerfaith. He looked across the paperless desktop.

"I have extremely sad news." She paused, then switched to a matter-of-fact tone. "Last night, I received notification that our recruiting officer in Canada...your friend Morrie George...is in a coma at Ottawa General."

Nick stared at Mrs. Fullerfaith. Morrie in a coma? *Can't be. He's too full of life.* A flash of adrenaline tingled through his body.

"Apparently Mr. George was arrested after someone spotted him playing hockey in the street with his children. He was released the same day." Her eyes misted over. "When his wife came home after her night shift at the hospital, she found her husband lying unconscious on the veranda"—Mrs. Fullerfaith swallowed—"with lacerations to his face, hands and head."

Nick was silent for a moment. "Who would...?" He trembled. He had realized all along something like this could happen, given what the world was like.

Mrs. Fullerfaith continued. "The word *traitor* was scrawled across the front door in red paint. The Hardinians claimed responsibility. Apparently, they committed this heinous act because Morrie had disclosed important facts about their organization when the police picked him up for questioning."

Nick's scalp tingled. He shot up from his chair, his fists clenched. "I want to... This..."

"The best way to deal with your rage, Nick, and avenge your friend's brutal assault is by immersing yourself even more fully in the School of Life. It's what Morrie would want for you."

Nick collapsed into his seat, his throat tight. "He...believed in me."

"An inspiration for us all. We must hope and pray for his recovery."

Nick leaned forward. "Can I call his wife? Let her know how sorry—

"This is a top-secret facility, Nick. All communication with the outside world is barred."

Nick leaned back and sat in silence, his eyes fixed on Mrs. Fullerfaith. "One thing I don't get. If he knew about this place, why in the world didn't he tell me? I had to—"

Severed Roots

"He thought you weren't ready. He wanted you to prove you wanted it badly enough. And now, Nick, I hope you'll make the best use of your new life here."

Nick left Mrs. Fullerfaith's office in a daze. Staring down at the blue tiles, he took small, dragging steps. The next thing he realized, he was in the cafeteria, occupying his usual seat in the dining area. He glanced around. Although it was early for lunch, a few silver-haired men and women were seated around him with coloured plastic trays. The smell of burritos, usually inviting, now sickened him. On impulse, Nick rose and walked to a table on the other side of the buffet counter, where a few people closer to his age were chatting. He stood before a small man seemingly in the company of his family. "Mind if I join you?"

"Not at all," the man replied, licking a dab of salsa off a finger. He glanced at the woman across the table before sliding over. "Name's Hal."

A teenage girl, seated at the end of the table between Hal and the woman, looked up. "Hey, you're Nick McTrick!"

Nick smiled, feeling some of the tension drain away.

"How'd you make that crayon change colour in your hand? It was so cool!"

"Magicians can't reveal their secrets, Becky," Hal said.

After a moment, Nick spoke up. "Sometimes, I wish I understood how other things work...like things in life."

The woman raised an eyebrow. "I'm Sheila, Hal's wife. And this is Becky, our precious daughter," she said, gesturing toward the teenager. "It's nice to have someone join us for lunch. We're honoured."

Nick took a seat next to Hal. A blue spiral notebook lay on the table, touching a pool of spilled salsa. "What's the pad for?"

"Oh, this?" She picked up the notebook while her daughter reached for a napkin. "I guess you haven't been here long?"

"About a month. Feels much shorter."

"Many residents keep a journal of what their kids teach them about life," said Hal. "Family is not just about parents raising their children. It's also about children raising their parents."

"What d'you mean?" Nick braced himself for more new ideas.

"Well, we're continually growing, improving ourselves. And our kids provide us with the challenges—the context—to do so. We learn to be more patient, more giving, more understanding."

Nick paused to take this in. He thought of Morrie's children, of Daniel kicking the legs of the dining room table and how calmly Morrie and Hanna had reacted to that incident.

Becky turned to Nick. "How come you don't have a tray, sir? You're not hungry?"

"Not very." Nick smiled tremulously. "I'm happy just being here with you. The last time I was with a family was…" Nick's eyes watered as he thought of Morrie's children, how they must miss their father. "It…it doesn't matter. There's a girl in that family—a tall girl—and her name is Becky, too."

They sat in silence. The hiss as someone opened a can of pop jolted Nick from his reverie.

"I wish I had a family," he said.

"Raised in a Children's Centre, were you?" Hal asked, though it sounded more like a statement than a question.

Nick nodded. "I feel…I don't know who I am."

"That doesn't surprise me," said Hal. "Much of our identity is based on relationships—we're a father, we're a son, we're a brother, we're a grandfather, we're an uncle."

"I'm none of those," Nick said. He swallowed hard.

Nick felt the weight of everyone's eyes on him. After a long silence, Sheila leaned in and squeezed his forearm. "It doesn't matter now," she whispered. "Even without a family, we're still like Lego pieces. We were designed for connection, and together we can build all kinds of great things." She smiled.

Nick lowered his eyes, deep in thought, his head bowed.

After a moment, he looked up. "I want a family. I want to know the proper way of raising children. To do that, I need to understand how my own upbringing shaped me."

"It'll take time," Sheila said. "Loads of time. I'd say half the residents here are on that same journey of discovery."

Nick pondered this. He indeed belonged in the Island House. Morrie would agree. Nick was determined to make each day of his journey count.

The next morning, Nick sprang out of bed, shaved, grabbed a Danish at the cafeteria, reconsidered and swapped it for a banana, then hurried down the stairs to the School of Life. He had enrolled in a course entitled "Parenting 101: Rediscovering the Lost Art."

"Every child needs an authority figure, someone to guide them," said Mrs. Serena, the white-haired teacher with overgrown front teeth that reminded Nick of Abbot the Rabbit he'd once used in his shows. "Parenting is a *sacred responsibility*. You're molding the next generation."

Severed Roots

Nick sat straighter in his chair.

"Here are some of the basics. Carry yourselves with dignity. Avoid discussing your personal problems with your children or even in front of them. Be friendly with your children, but don't mistake them for your friends. You need to command respect—not to satisfy your ego, but for *their* benefit, so they'll feel secure."

A man with a well-trimmed goatee and East Asian features yelled out in broken English, "But how to make your children respect you?"

The instructor tucked in her chin and looked at the man over her glasses.

"Sir, you must constantly work on yourself to become the best person you can be. At the same time, encourage your children from the earliest age to speak in a pleasant tone of voice, not to interrupt you, to address you as Dad, Father, or the like—never by your first name—and not to contradict you overtly."

Nick recalled Morrie and Hanna's son kicking the table legs during dinner and how they used words to resolve his outburst. It worked that time, but did it always work? Nick's hand shot up. "Is it okay to spank children if they're naughty?" The words tumbled out before he realized how insensitive his question must have sounded. Men controlled and abused children throughout history by spanking them and worse.

The instructor's eyes lit up. "Thank you for asking that, sir. Every interaction with your children must be motivated by love. You must never punish or even threaten punishment when you're angry. Wait until you calm down, and then think over the situation logically, objectively, always asking yourself, *What is in the best interest of my child?*"

Mrs. Serena paced the floor. "For generations, parents simply beat their children, not realizing there was a better way..."

Nick tried to imagine being a father. In the Island House, parenthood was almost expected. And if he were a father, there would have to be a mother—someone who loved children. She would have to love them so much she'd be prepared to make the tremendous sacrifices a *sacred responsibility* entailed.

An image of Beatrice, with her large, gentle eyes and wide smile, appeared in Nick's head. Beatrice would certainly relish being a mother. She and Nick could learn parenting skills together. *Hmm*...how many children would they have? One? Two? Four, like Morrie and Hanna? Beatrice was still young, not yet thirty.

My God! When's her birthday? He glanced at his watch. August 2. *She may already be dead!*

Nick left the classroom and hurried along the corridor, breaking out in a sweat. He needed to talk to Mrs. Fullerfaith. But how would he approach her? Dunn's words came back to him. *"Once you enter the Island House, you will not be allowed to leave."*

He bolted up the stairs, almost tripping over his bulky running shoes, and barged into the executive director's suite. Perspiration pasted his T-shirt to his back. There she was, looking at some sheets of paper. Nick apologized and spoke rapidly.

When he finished, Mrs. Fullerfaith said, "Your friend Beatrice sounds like a perfect candidate for the Island House. However, as you know, we can't let you leave."

"But you must make an exception!" Nick protested. "Saving a life should trump security considerations."

Mrs. Fullerfaith raised an index finger. "That's a good point—a very good point. But we don't know if your friend is still alive, do we? We also don't know if you could convince her to come to a place she's never been to and would never be able to leave."

"I'm sure she'd come, after I describe this place to her, what it can offer—"

Mrs. Fullerfaith held up a hand. "Talking about this place to anyone on the outside is forbidden. Think about it. If Beatrice—for whatever reason—chose not to come here, her knowledge of the Island House would pose a threat to our collective survival."

"Beatrice would never tell anyone."

"We can't take any chances. If the government shut this place down, it would be devastating for the eight hundred people who live here."

"But didn't *Morrie* know—"

"Our recruitment officers are carefully vetted and intensively trained." Mrs. Fullerfaith leaned toward Nick. "It breaks my heart, Nick. But I'm afraid the answer is no, you can't go to Beatrice."

Her refusal felt like a door slammed in his face. He sank into the chair opposite Mrs. Fullerfaith. He closed his eyes for a few seconds, then snapped them open.

"What if you sent someone with me? A security escort? I could pretend to be a supervised offender on a pass."

"Esmeralda is a maximum-security facility. It doesn't grant temporary leaves of absence. To do so would raise suspicion. And now, if you'll kindly excuse me—"

"Can you at least let me call her, so I can find out if she's still alive?" Nick grabbed the edges of the desk, squeezing tightly. "Please—I must know."

"All telephone and electronic communication to and from the Island House is blocked," Mrs. Fullerfaith said, her face now stern. "Only I can bypass the security, and there's good reason for that. If you were to phone Beatrice, then what? If she didn't reply, you'd want to go to her. And if she did reply, you couldn't reveal where or what the Island House is."

Nick rose from his chair and slammed an open hand on the executive director's desk. "Dammit! I never signed any contract with you. You can't keep me here!"

Mrs. Fullerfaith looked Nick in the eye. "Signing a piece of paper is not essential. There was a verbal understanding. Nick, I'm warning you. Any attempt to escape will be met with a severe beating." Mrs. Fullerfaith held out a hand. "I'm sorry."

Nick stormed to his quarters, slammed the door behind him and threw himself onto his bed. He breathed heavily, moaning from time to time.

Then, something occurred to him.

He sat up. Had he been overreacting? Hadn't he agreed—even if it was only verbally—to the security conditions? And, really, how likely was it that Beatrice would set herself on fire? People said alarming things when they were distressed, and since the incident in Amazon Mall, she hadn't mentioned her intentions to him again. Nick himself had experienced suicidal urges over the years, and here he was, still alive.

Even so, he felt unsettled. What if Mrs. Fullerfaith's perspective was wrong? Was he simply to trust her judgment because she ran the Island House, which supposedly was grounded in wisdom and moral truths?

Nick spent the rest of the day in his room contemplating the situation, while nibbling on veggies he kept at his bedside. He didn't report to the Duty Station for his daily cleaning job, and thankfully no one came looking for him.

Shortly after ten in the evening, a polite knock came at Nick's door. When he opened it, a vaguely familiar face stared at him with apologetic eyes.

"My name iz Dmitri Ivanov. May I come in? It is important." He spoke slowly.

The Russian fellow, from one of the classes. "Sure. I'm Nick. Sorry, there's only the bed—"

Dmitri waved a hand. "You sit. I stand." He stepped inside the room.

Nick hesitantly sat down on the edge of his bed and looked up at his visitor—a robust, clean-shaven man sporting a beaded necklace over a black T-shirt with an unusually low neckline. The man was probably in his early thirties, like Nick.

"Zis morning I saw you leave executive director office. Your face look like train hit you. I know you new to Island House. Are you happy being prisoner?"

"Prisoner?"

"We are all." He looked around the room.

Nick wondered whether Dmitri had a similar reason for wanting to leave.

Severed Roots

"Well," Nick said. "This place is top secret. We all agreed to the condition, didn't we? That once we enter here, we're not supposed to leave."

Dmitri's jaw tightened. "I don't mean prisoner in body. I mean prisoner in mind." He tapped a forefinger against his temple. "*Yazyk khorosho podvyeshen.* Old Russian idiom: Ze teachers know how to talk."

Nick stood. "Look, Dmitri, I happen to find the lectures fascinating, and I'm learning a lot of new concepts. The school is optional. No one's forcing you to attend."

"Yes. Zey are cunning."

"Cunning...?"

"Zey make optional. Zey make you believe you free to think ze way you want. Zey even encourage questions. Each question iz another opportunity for zem to brainwash you more."

"You're saying that asking questions is a problem?" Nick felt the temperature quickly rise in his body.

"It iz *illusion* of free thought." He narrowed his eyes at Nick. "I see you in hallway with kids—you magician, yes? You understand about illusion."

Nick didn't reply.

Dmitri crossed his arms in front of his chest. "People think zey are free. But me, I look through both eyes and know what iz real situation."

Nick furrowed his brow. "Can you give an example?"

"I can give many example." He planted his feet in a wide stance and tugged at his T-shirt. "I want to remove my clothes like I used to do back home in Krasnodar. Sit in cafeteria naked. Good for health of body. On second day in Island House, two big men grab me and warn me not to do again. Still, I did again. Zey gave me lashes." He lifted his T-shirt and twisted his torso, displaying a raised, foot-long pink scar on his side. "Mrs. Fullerfaith said if I do third time, she send me as prisoner in Esmeralda, in mental health unit. I say to her, prisoner here, prisoner zer, what difference?"

Nick wasn't sure he agreed with Dmitri's perspective. He recalled the teacher in a recent class introducing the concept of modesty. "Hmm. Is it possible some residents feel uncomfortable seeing you naked?"

"Zat's *zer* problem!" He jabbed a finger in Nick's face. "Zey are brainwashed to think human body shameful."

Dmitri's blue eyes turned hard. "These teachers think zer iz is only one right way to live. You have to get married—a man to a woman. Not a man to two women or a woman to two men. Not a man to a man or a woman to a woman. Those all bad options. Where zey get these rules? Only *zer* way is correct! Zer is no democracy, no freedom. Everyone nice to you if you think like zem. But if you think different, zey rule with iron fist."

"Why did you join this place?"

Dmitri thrust his chest out and pointed a thumb to it. "I wanted to choose how I live my life—not be told by Advisor, by Russian government, by no one. And what do I discover? Totalitarianism here just as bad. Treating us like children. From one bad place to different bad place."

Nick wanted to continue the conversation, but his head was spinning, and he was afraid it would trigger a migraine. "Let me think about what you said, Dmitri."

"Yes, Nick. You keep eyes wide open. You new here. If you start feel like prisoner, you find me in room 205. You good magician. Maybe we plan escape together, eh?"

After Dmitri left, Nick ran a hand through his hair. *What a confusing world!*

He stretched out on his mattress and rubbed his temples.

Zer iz no democracy.

Yet, in the world at large, there was democracy—misguided people electing misguided leaders to make misguided laws.

It took him a long time to fall asleep.

The following morning, Nick got up late. As he stepped out to use the communal bathroom, he found a folded note under his door. It was from Mrs. Fullerfaith, asking to see him.

Nick's heartbeat raced. *She'll probably give me lashes for acting out yesterday in her office.*

And as soon as the lashes are over, I'll go find Dmitri.

CHAPTER TWENTY-TWO

"Listen," Mrs. Fullerfaith said, as soon as Nick, bleary-eyed and unshaven, sat down in her office. "Everything I've heard about you over the past weeks, in addition to the screening by Mr. Dunn, points to a young man of high moral integrity. Still, given how much is at stake for the Island House, I needed to be extra sure."

Nick looked up, a fluttering in his belly.

"The fact that you became angry at the prospect of not being able to save a human being's life assured me of your inherent goodness. The fact that you proposed a security escort further convinced me your motives are sincere. And the fact that you ultimately accepted my decision and did not lash out excessively tells me you are mature and responsible." She stood and gestured toward the door. "I consulted with my executive team last night. I grant you permission to go."

Nick's chest swelled with exhilaration and relief.

"There are some conditions. Your phone stays with us. You must not talk about the Island House to anyone, including your friend, until she arrives here. You have forty-eight hours. If you can't convince her to come with you, you must immediately return."

"I promise," said Nick.

"And one more thing. You must not visit anyone else, including Morrie or his family."

"Why not?"

"In case anyone questions you about your connection to him. We can't take any chances. Now go—and may God protect you."

An hour later, Nick was heading to Des Moines on his bike, his chin high. He'd been escorted through a labyrinth of winding staircases, dark corridors, security doors and fences, and he appreciated being outside again. The ride was largely downhill and the midmorning air cool. Thoughts of Beatrice chased each other through his head.

What can I say to make her come away with me? The Island House is so different from everything she knows.

The bike wobbled as it skittered on a patch of loose gravel, and he guided it to a smoother path.

Will she trust me? Should I tell her that once we get to this mystery place, she can never leave?

At the most terrifying question of all, he shivered. *Is she still alive?*

Nick tensed as the wind picked up, blowing in dark clouds that turned the morning sky an ominous grey. As he neared Des Moines Central Station, cold drops of rain soaked into his shirt and sweatpants.

He entered the station, and a moment later his stomach rumbled. The enticing aroma from the food vendors' stands made him regret not taking a few extra minutes at the Island House to pack snacks for the trip. He'd been too eager to get to Beatrice. Now he couldn't buy anything to eat as he barely had enough money for the train ticket back to Ottawa.

He shrugged. *Good to lose weight anyway.*

During the long train ride, Nick thought a lot about Dmitri. The Russian fellow was bold, questioning, independent-minded. Rare traits in a mankey. What if Dmitri was right—that the Island House, with its School of Life, was a cult? If so, it would be a colossal mistake for Nick to bring Beatrice there. "From one bad place to different bad place," as Dmitri would say. Once at the Island House, she wouldn't be allowed to leave.

Nick's head spun in circles every time he considered the matter. Did he have the moral right to determine another human being's fate? Play God? Perhaps he should turn back. Eventually, Nick decided it was wise to take things one step at a time. *I must go to Beatrice if only to make sure she doesn't kill herself.*

When Nick finally arrived at his basement apartment, it was past 2:30 a.m. His key still worked, which meant the lock hadn't been changed. *Morrie. He or Hanna must have paid my landlord.* Nick grinned, feeling his eyes brim with tears. *Oh, Morrie, please get well.*

It was too early in the morning to go to Beatrice. No point banging on her door. She'd need to be well rested for the possible long journey ahead. He peeled off his damp clothes and smelly socks, made himself a double-decker peanut butter sandwich with bread he found in the freezer, ate half and collapsed onto the mattress. Before he allowed sleep to overtake him, he reached over to his clock and set the alarm for 7:30 a.m.

When the alarm sounded, it took Nick a few seconds to remember where he was. Once he became oriented, it occurred to him with a jolt that he was a fool to have returned to his apartment. The police were surely looking for him, and his flat would be an obvious place to watch. In fact, had Mrs. Fullerfaith known that Nick could be wanted by the police, she surely wouldn't have allowed him to return to Ottawa.

In a fit of panic, Nick jumped out of bed, threw on an old pair of jeans and a T-shirt, and rushed outside with his bike. He looked around. A few vehicles were parked on the street. Traffic was light.

Nick pedalled quickly, travelling several blocks in one direction, then making four successive right turns while intermittently stopping, looking over his shoulder or temporarily changing direction. Fifteen minutes later, satisfied that he was not being followed, he proceeded to Beatrice's apartment.

It took a while for her door to open.

"Nick!" Beatrice said, jerking her head backward.

Thank God she's alive. Nick's heart danced in his chest.

Beatrice took a step back, looking him over. "Where've you been? What're you doing here?" Her eyes were wider than he'd ever seen them.

Nick opened his mouth to begin the speech he had prepared but shut it when he realized how haggard and weary Beatrice looked. "Can I come in?"

She hesitated, then opened the door wider and let him inside.

Her place was no longer the orderly dwelling Nick had visited in the past. Discarded clothing and shoes formed a trail leading to her bedroom. Her clay figurines had grown in number, and muddy water from her pottery table had dripped onto the floor and furniture and left smears. Dust covered everything.

Beatrice's eyes slid over him as she shook her head. "Nick, I barely recognize you. You've changed."

Nick shrugged. His clothes were looser, and he had more energy. But the one who had really changed was her. It was clear she'd fallen into depression. The possibility that she would take her life was very real. He definitely needed to take her away with him.

"No, really. You look taller. And so confident! Whatever you're into, I could use some of it."

Nick smiled. She had just given him the perfect opening.

He reached out and took her hand. "I want to take you to an incredible place, a place where you'll be happy." His heart pounded with excitement. "But we've got to go today. Pack some clothes and personal items. Only the bare essentials, whatever you can fit in your knapsack. I'll meet you back here in two hours. You'll need your bike and all your money."

Beatrice stared at Nick. "Where're we going?"

"Just do everything as fast as you can." He had anticipated this question and borrowing from his years of misdirection as a magician, had formulated a non-sensical image to disorient Beatrice and delay further questioning. "I'll explain later, before the flowerpots get flooded!" *Now to get out of here before she recovers from that one.* He exited Beatrice's house, hopped onto his bike with such force he almost fell over, and began pedaling in the direction of Ottawa General Hospital.

After rounding the corner, Nick braked gently. Should he actually do it? On the one hand, Mrs. Fullerfaith had given him a clear order not to visit anyone other than Beatrice. On the other, he pictured Hanna and the four children surrounding Morrie's hospital bed, their eyes red and puffy from endless crying, telling Nick how much they missed their father, praying for him to regain consciousness. Nick wanted to be there, crying and praying with them. And oddly, the fact that he had no idea how to pray didn't matter.

He pushed his shoulders back. *No, I'll do what's right, not what I feel like doing. As much as it pains me, I must keep my promise to Mrs. Fullerfaith.*

The morning air was still, and low-lying clouds blanketed the sky. A drone hovered in the distance. Nick glanced at his watch: eight fifteen. He had almost two hours before he'd have to go back for Beatrice. Should he go to her now? He wanted to be with her, but she'd inundate him with questions. It could slow her packing, maybe diminish her resolve. Besides, he had told her he'd see her in two hours. If he didn't follow through on his word, she'd have less confidence in other things he'd tell her.

He looked around. A few elderly women were lined up in front of a hardware store. A large bulldog walked ahead of a young woman, pulling at its leash. Two middle-aged mankeys with long, scruffy beards sat cross-legged on the sidewalk, holding up a piece of cardboard on which a few words were scrawled: "Am Nothing, Got Nothing."

Nick sighed. He didn't miss Ottawa. This was the city he'd grown up in, the only city he knew, but he'd never really felt connected to its people, its landscape, its history. Maybe the same was true for everyone in his generation, having spent most of their childhood within the lonely walls of Children's Centres.

Nick got off his bike and searched his pockets. He approached the two panhandlers, crouched down and dropped the little bit of money he had left—a few coins—equally in each of their cups. "Change your sign. You're not nothing," he said to them sternly. "You're somebody."

Their faces remained blank.

St. Theresa Roman Catholic Church stood across the street. Nick gazed at its vertical structure, its white steeple, the segments of stained glass radiating from the large circular window above the main entrance. He thought of Angelina and felt a lump in his throat. *Is she still alive? Did she find serenity through her Catholic faith?*

Nick had never been inside a house of worship. On impulse, he biked across the street and approached the edifice. After leaning his bike against a nearby tree and glancing around to make sure no one would steal it, he took a deep breath and entered the church.

He was greeted by a musty smell, mixed with the fragrance of candle wax and some sweet aroma he didn't recognize. The scent relaxed him as he proceeded into the sanctuary. It was vacant except for an old man who stood in front of the altar, mumbling something incoherent and moaning intermittently. His upper body appeared unusually rigid.

Nick stood at the rear of the centre aisle, blinking, before turning slowly to take in his surroundings—the dizzying artistic details in the stained-glass windows, the Nativity scene animating the ceramic mural, the imposing wooden crucifix, the statues of religious figures lining the walls, and other furnishings he couldn't identify. He had stepped inside an alien, ethereal landscape, one that had been familiar to his ancestors but was unknown to him.

His ancestors. Italian. Catholic, probably. They or someone like them had erected this magnificent building because they believed in...what?

Nick felt an urge to pray and tried to envision how that was done. After a few minutes, he shrugged, closed his eyes, and clasped his hands together.

He slowly took in a full breath and exhaled deeply, feeling the tension in his shoulders melt away.

Angelina, you've kept in touch with me since I was a child at the Children's Centre. Why? What made you want to befriend me, a mere mankey?

He placed a fist against his heart.

Angelina—I regret not visiting you in the hospital. When I had that opportunity, I squandered it. Now I want to visit you but can't. Angelina, if you're still alive, I hope when your time is up, you will go peacefully, with the least possible discomfort.

Nick opened his eyes. The old man from the altar was hobbling toward him. A scrawny mankey in tattered clothes, with a heavily lined face and misty eyes.

"Don't mean to disturb you, brother, if you're in the middle of supplication." His voice was feeble.

"It's okay." Nick wasn't sure what "supplication" was but didn't want to appear ignorant.

"I'm Max. The caretaker. I like to greet visitors. Not many at this hour." He spoke haltingly, as if he needed time to rest between words.

"My name's Nick."

"A pleasure." He offered his bony hand. "What brings you here?"

"I came to...pray."

"'Course. I didn't think you came to play poker." The white whiskers on his chin danced as he chuckled. "Welcome to the House of God." He lifted his hands upward and out, while his upper body remained rigid.

Severed Roots

Nick pressed his lips into a thin line.

The old man winced. "You're not a believer?"

"A believer? Honestly, I prefer to question rather than to believe."

"Why's that?" said the caretaker, edging closer to Nick. The smell of cough drops leaked from the corner of his mouth.

"There's a danger in believing."

"A danger? What kind of danger?"

"Once you believe something, you may stop questioning; you may stop growing."

"Ahh...so you believe...in questioning." The old man looked away. "I was like you, for a very long time. Now it might be too late for me to be saved."

Nick raised his eyebrows.

The old man cast his watery eyes on Nick. "I'm eighty-two—too frail for the operation."

"Operation?"

"To become a woman."

Nick grimaced. "What does becoming a woman have to do with being saved?"

"Everything." His face sagged.

Nick did not respond.

"You don't get it, do you?" he continued, his voice stronger. "Jesus came as a man. He died for our sins. Why do you reckon Jesus came as a man and not as a woman?"

Nick fiddled with his shirtsleeve. "Because sins were perpetrated mostly by men?"

"Bingo. Unfortunately, men are damned even if they are believers. Women can surrender to God, but we men can't. Not fully, at least. It's not in our nature to be submissive. I remember..." His gaze became unfocused.

"Remember what?"

"How it used to be, before the chemical injections turned men into mankeys. The male aggression. The toxicity. It was awful."

Nick crossed his arms. "Do you think the Rite of Passage is a good thing?"

"'Course, but it ain't enough. Any man's surrendering to the Lord is tainted by ego, by a subconscious desire to dominate." The old man leaned forward and peered into Nick's eyes. His watery eyes became even more watery. "I'm doomed, Nick. Doomed, doomed, doomed." His whole body trembled.

Nick placed a hand on the old man's shoulder. "Listen, Max," he said firmly. "Maybe what you've been taught is wrong. Always remember there are different views and perspectives—about life, about death, about everything."

"Is that what you believe?"

"I know it. It could be a tiny number of people who think differently from everyone else, and maybe they have to go underground in order to be left alone and be able to teach their ideas to others. The important thing is we must never stop questioning. Never."

The man stared at Nick in silence. Soon, his upper body relaxed. "Thank you, brother," he said. "I needed to hear that... I will now go in peace."

"Go where?"

"I've lived my life."

Nick shuddered. "You can continue!"

The caretaker smiled, shaking his head. "I'm afraid that would be 'lingering'."

Nick lifted a hand up and then let it fall. "Sorry, I didn't mean to—"

"No worries, brother. You meant well."

Nick left the caretaker, eyes downcast, and went outside.

His bike was gone.

Nick's eyes darted every which way, until he spotted it across the street. The two panhandlers whom Nick had given money to earlier were walking away with his green hybrid bike!

Nick ran after them. As he neared the intersection, the light turned red, and the moving cars made crossing the street impossible.

"Hey, that's my bike. You're stealing my bike!" Nick yelled across the street, flailing his arms while struggling to catch his breath. The panhandlers turned their heads briefly, then continued walking a little faster.

"Come back here! Thieves!"

He needed his bike. How else could he take Beatrice to the Island House?

As soon as there was a small break in the flow of traffic, he stepped off the curb and began to cross cautiously, only to be greeted by an ear-splitting chorus of honks and, seconds later, a wailing siren.

When he finally reached the other side, frazzled, the thieves were no longer in sight.

They must have turned the corner.

Fifteen feet away, two policewomen, likely in their twenties, were getting out of their cruiser. "What's your name?" asked the one with the bright yellow turban, as they approached Nick.

Nick's heart hammered in his chest. If he disclosed his identity, the officers would check it against the police database and likely learn that there was a warrant for his arrest. His goal of returning to the Island House would be shattered.

"I-I'm sorry I stepped through traffic like that," said Nick. "It was a mankeyish thing to do. But those crooks walked off with my bike, and I wanted to catch them while I still could." Nick pointed in the direction the panhandlers had been heading.

Neither officer turned to look. The turbaned one spoke again. "Your name, please."

Nick considered giving a false name, but he carried his ID in his pocket. The officers might search him, then arrest him for attempting to obstruct justice or something like that.

"I prefer to keep my identity private."

The second policewoman, slim and sporting multiple nose rings, nodded. "You have the right not to talk to us. I'm Constable Burns and this is Constable Sidhu. This event is being recorded with our body cams. You have a right to a free copy of the video recordings. You also have a right to a lawyer and to a PTSD therapist. And should you feel unduly harassed by us, you can file a complaint with the Ottawa Police Complaints Commission." She handed Nick a colourful pamphlet entitled, "Know Your Rights: A Guide for Mankeys."

Officer Sidhu cleared her throat. "You disobeyed traffic rules and endangered public safety. Unless you have a diagnosed mental condition that could excuse your actions, we need to know your identity in order to charge you. If you do not provide that information, we will have no choice but to welcome you into our custody."

Nick's head was spinning. He had to get away from these cops. But how? If he ran, they'd probably overtake him. And they had batons, so he wouldn't be able to fend them off.

He looked toward the intersection, pretending to be lost in thought. The light was green.

Opportunity knocks.

"Here's my ID" Nick reached into his pocket, pulled out his Ministry ID card and held it up with its back side facing the officers. In a flash, he slid the card over his ring and middle fingers with his thumb. His pinky and index finger guided the card smoothly. It was now hidden behind his hand.

The officers' eyes widened.

"Oh, it's right there on the sidewalk, just behind you," Nick said, pointing with his other hand.

The officers turned and looked down. In that instant, Nick threw his full weight into the nose-ringed officer so she fell backward into the turbaned officer, and both of them tumbled onto the pavement. Quickly regaining his balance, he turned toward the intersection. The light was now yellow. Nick tore across the street. Just as he reached the other side, the cross traffic started to move.

Nick didn't want to waste precious seconds looking back but hoped the two officers were not hurt too badly. He continued running like a madman, past

Severed Roots

the church, reaching the next street, turning left, continuing to the end, making further random turns and running and running until he could no longer breathe.

CHAPTER TWENTY-THREE

Throughout the train ride, Nick fought the growing urge to tell Beatrice where they were going. His pulse quickened every time he imagined her excitement when they reached the Island House. He'd finally be able to share the classes and the new perspective he'd gained. He'd show her the gigantic playground, the children and families. He'd point out the health clinic and explain the procedures to reverse men's infertility, and he could tell her about the medication he had started on. But all this was still in the future. He wouldn't go against Mrs. Fullerfaith's directive.

At Des Moines Central Station, Beatrice bought egg-salad sandwiches and yogurt for the two of them. They sat across from each other inside a twenty-four-hour fast-food outlet. Beatrice's old yellow bike leaned against the nearby wall, next to Nick's new blue mountain bike that Beatrice had hastily purchased for him.

Severed Roots

It was 3:40 a.m. After a few bites of the sandwiches, both acknowledged they were more tired than hungry.

"So," Beatrice perked up her body posture. "Where are we going?" she asked for the umpteenth time.

Nick swallowed. "I can't tell you." His voice wavered. "Like I said, I'm not allowed to tell you until we get there."

Beatrice leaned back, crossed her arms, and studied Nick's face. "Y'know, I must be insane leaving everything behind—my home, my life—and following you. On the other hand, I was planning to leave it all behind anyway..."

Nick stared at Beatrice.

"...next Wednesday." Her tone was flat.

Nick let out a long sigh of relief. *I returned for her in the nick of time.* He smiled to himself at his little word play.

"Anyway," Beatrice continued, nibbling her sandwich. "Wherever you're taking me, I think I'll be happier. Otherwise, you wouldn't take me there, would you?"

"Of course not." The only thing that would make Beatrice happier was becoming a mother, which the Island House would facilitate, and he didn't want the conversation to go in that direction. He tried to change the topic. "So, did you tell your supervisor you won't be coming in for a while?"

"Didn't need to. I quit five days ago."

Nick fidgeted on the hard plastic seat. "Uh, I guess you didn't really like your job." *Ape-brain! She quit because she planned to set herself on fire.*

"The job was okay. But the women in the lab are all airheads."

"I see. Had you considered changing jobs?"

Beatrice shifted in her seat. "For years I thought about applying for a position in human manufacturing. If I managed to get accepted, my plan was to wait till a month before the baby was due, then run away to northern Ontario and raise the child myself."

Nick laughed and immediately regretted it. He vaguely remembered Karla mentioning such plans being made by women who suffered from severe motherhood syndrome. "How would you have survived?"

"Sometimes I fantasized about finding a man who was skilled in wilderness survival. Someone who liked the idea of raising a child. We'd live there together, in the bush, the three of us. We'd build a log cabin, hunt, grow food."

"Do you think such men exist?" Nick asked. "I mean, there are the Hardinians—"

Beatrice squirmed. "The Hardinians don't love children. They don't love women either. They only care about themselves."

Severed Roots

Ahh. The Hardinians want the family unit back, but just so women and children can serve them. Nick's thoughts wandered to Angelina's father. Angelina had said her father believed he had the right to control every aspect of his wife's life—the type of clothes she wore, how she spent their money, who she socialized with. Maybe if Angelina's father had been born a generation later, he'd have joined Monsieur Hardin's newly minted organization and become a prominent Hardinian.

"Oh, by the way," Beatrice said. "I got a call from your friend Morrie a couple of weeks ago. I figured you must have given him my number."

Good old Morrie. Must have called to check up on her after I told him about her suicide plan. Morrie… Nick's insides twisted as he pictured his friend lying motionless on a gurney in a tangle of tubes and wires, unable to lift a finger. "What did he want?"

"He said he enjoyed meeting me at your magic show and would like to get to know me better. Odd, isn't it—for a mankey to say that to a woman? And—listen to this—he even asked when my birthday was. You sure have unusual friends, Nick."

Nick lifted his chin. "Did the two of you get together?"

"We were supposed to. But for some reason, he never returned my calls."

Nego Huzcotoq

No point telling her he was brutally attacked by Hardinians and is lying in a coma. It will only upset her.

When they had given up on trying to finish their meals, Nick and Beatrice collected their bikes. As they crossed the concourse on their way out of the station, Nick spotted the man who had given him directions to the Island House. He sat cross-legged on the floor, nursing a cigarette. He looked the same—long hair, coffee-stained T-shirt, glazed eyes.

Could he be a plant for the Island House? Nick wouldn't put it past Mrs. Fullerfaith to have assigned the unlikely looking mankey the job of giving seekers directions. Nick pursed his lips, wondering whether to approach the man or not. He wanted to say thank you for having helped him.

No, he'd better not. He couldn't risk blowing the man's cover. Besides, Mrs. Fullerfaith's directive was to avoid talking to anyone about the Island House. Without slowing his pace, Nick continued walking toward the exit with Beatrice.

They mounted their bikes. It was just past four in the morning, the air was crisp, and a crescent moon illuminated the cloudless sky. Nick felt good.

After forty minutes of pedaling, the ground beneath him shook, first subtly, then vigorously. He looked up, and the same thing was happening to the trees. Nick's wheels wobbled.

"Are you okay?" Beatrice shouted from a few feet behind.

Pain. All he could feel was pain. Crushing pain, like a stack of bricks pressing down on his skull and squeezing his brain. Beatrice shouted something else, but he couldn't understand.

Nick braked and almost fell off his bike. He stumbled to the side of the dirt road. He dropped onto the soft earth and rested his head on his arm, his hands grasping his skull.

The world is nothing but searing pain and pressure.

Pain and pressure.

I am pain, and the world is pain, and I and the world are one.

Something new is happening. My head is lifted, moved and placed onto a softer surface. Small hands and fingers spread across my scalp. The fingers are moving, slowly, steadily, in small circles around my ears.

As long as the hands are there, my head will not explode.

I am safe.

A tingling sensation mixes with the pain.

The pressure eases.

"Does this help, Nick? Should I get you some water?"

Nick opened his eyes. He tilted his head back and saw Beatrice gazing at him in the soft glow of predawn, her round dimpled face framed by wavy golden hair. His head was in her lap.

He managed a weak smile. She smiled back.

"You were out for ten minutes. I got really scared."

Nick propped himself onto his elbows. He and Beatrice needed to get back on the road. He tried to sit up, then dropped his head back into the soft cushion of her lap. "I'm dizzy."

"Must be from exhaustion—coming to get me and then all this traveling." Beatrice leaned over, and he could see her better.

"When you were massaging my head, it felt good."

They rested in silence.

"Beatrice, if we weren't together—like now—and I ended up in the hospital, would you visit me?"

"To massage your scalp?"

Nick smiled slightly. "To keep me company."

"What do you think?"

"I don't know. What if you were busy? Say it was in the middle of your workday—"

"Still, why wouldn't I?" She sounded irritated.

"Imagine we lived in a world where we could be related—and you're my sister or my, uh, wife or something—would you visit me?"

"And risk being arrested?" Beatrice laughed. "Seriously, if we were family, I'd visit you because I *had* to, not necessarily because I'd want to."

"Is that good?"

"It would give you a sense of security, wouldn't it? Knowing that even if I didn't want to, I would still visit you."

Nick took a few deep breaths. The air smelled of cow dung. A film of dried sweat tickled his forehead. "But how can they be free?"

"What?"

"How can family members be free if they're not given a choice whether to take care of one another?"

Beatrice was silent for a long moment. "Nick, ultimately the goal of freedom is to be happy, to live a meaningful and fulfilling life, and you can't do that if you're self-centered, can you?"

Nick looked down at his hands. He had said something similar to Dunn when the man refused to help him.

"So," Beatrice continued. "Family members don't *choose* their obligations toward each other—they inherit them. What they choose is whether to fulfill or neglect their obligations."

Nick reflected on Beatrice's words while they rested in silence. A breeze caressed his face, and it occurred to him with a kick of satisfaction that he and Beatrice were sharing the same breeze.

"Beatrice? Remember that day in the mall? I was lined up outside Simple Wear, waiting to buy new pink slippers, and I spotted you on a bench."

"I was hoping you would abandon the queue. And you did!"

"I didn't want to lose my place. I only left because I felt I had to, not because I wanted to."

"Hey, Nick! That's what a family member would do!" Beatrice chuckled.

Nick squeezed his eyes shut. "But I stopped short. In the end, when I knew you needed me most—when you told me how you would celebrate your thirtieth birthday—I abandoned you. I was afraid. I don't know of what, but deep down I was afraid. I've felt horrible to this day." Nick opened his eyes. They were burning. "I-I'm so sorry. Beatrice, this is why we're here now. Ultimately, it's because of that incident in the mall."

Beatrice leaned over and kissed Nick on the forehead. "You always want to do the right thing, Nick. It's what I like most about you."

Nick felt his neck muscles relaxing and then had a jolt of inspiration. "Will you forgive me?"

Beatrice grinned widely. "Of course. Remember? We're 'family'!"

Once Nick was able to stand without his head hurting and without feeling nauseous, he said, "We've gotta get going," and mounted his bike.

Severed Roots

Beatrice shook her head. "Nick, maybe we should go back to town. We can find a room and you could get some rest. I'm concerned about you. Maybe you threw a blood clot or had a ministroke or—"

"No, I'm fine. It's important we keep moving. Just get on your bike. Trust me."

She cocked her head. "Okay, Nick. I'm sure you know what's best."

Those words surprised Nick more than Beatrice's ready agreement to accompany him on this trip. As they pedaled up the road, he mulled them over. Beatrice had no idea where Nick was taking her, so she already trusted him. But for Nick—a mankey—to "know what's best" sounded strange, coming from a woman. He liked hearing her say it, but he was also concerned about her state of mind.

Beatrice drew up alongside him. "Nick, you've really changed. You seem so assertive. I feel like you know what you want. If this place you're taking me to has helped you that much, I can't wait to get there."

They arrived at Esmeralda Penitentiary in the late morning. When Beatrice saw the sign on the fence, she looked at Nick with questioning eyes. Nick assured her he'd explain soon, and she gave him a doubtful nod.

A drone hovering a few hundred meters away suddenly receded. They proceeded through the gates and left their bikes near the main entrance. Although they were exhausted, Nick started telling Beatrice everything. Beatrice gave him a wider smile than he'd ever seen. She grinned and bounced up and down on her feet as they waited to be let inside.

"Pinch me, Nick. I must be dreaming. To be able to get married and have a family! Be a mother, raise children!" She touched his arm. "I can't believe this is really happening. I'm so excited."

The warden and Dunn met with them, assessed Beatrice and had her agree to the security conditions, which she did without hesitation.

As Nick and Beatrice emerged from the tunnel into the Island House, Beatrice quickened her step. She was radiant, and Nick's heart tugged at seeing the colour in her cheeks. She looked so beautiful. Beatrice started to follow the guide who'd been assigned to take her to the women's quarters, but after a few steps in that direction, she turned back and ran to Nick, hugged him and whispered in his ear. "Thank you, Nick." With a quick kiss on the cheek, she was gone.

Nick watched as Beatrice and her guide walked away, and memories of past hugs filled him with warmth. But he also felt something new. He hadn't wanted to let Beatrice go. It felt good to surround her with his arms, her warm body pressed against his. He wanted to keep her safe.

Severed Roots

There was something else. A feeling he couldn't identify, deep down. It was intense, making his heart beat faster. Hugs were special, but this latest hug held a promise of something new.

An alarm woke Nick from an afternoon nap in his room. Seconds later, a solemn voice came through a loudspeaker.

"Ladies and gentlemen, this is Mrs. Fullerfaith. I am sorry to inform you that a dozen government officials from Canada's Ministry of Tomorrow, followed by US and World Federation law enforcement officers and agents from the international media, have descended on Esmeralda Penitentiary and gained access to the Island House."

The intercom squealed, and after a brief tapping sound, her voice resumed. "They have disabled our telecom jamming system. So more officials are expected to arrive throughout the evening."

Nick was wide awake, sitting on his mattress and clutching the edge with cold hands.

"They may arrest men and women who are in a relationship or who have children."

She cleared her throat. "Please remain calm. Ladies and gentlemen, all classes, social activities and nonessential work are suspended.

"Canada's chief of enforcement has agreed to hold a conference with me, my staff, and the members of the community in the main social hall at six this evening, at which time we will explain our position. Do not be afraid. I urge everyone to attend with your children and be prepared to speak as witnesses."

Silence fell as the intercom snapped off.

Nick slumped over, his face cradled in his hands. It could be no coincidence that this was happening right after his return to the Island House. But what was the connection? Had someone followed him? No, that couldn't be—he was careful about hiding his tracks.

He slammed his hand against his skull and jumped up.

Beatrice! The Ministry must have planted a GPS microchip on her!

He paced the room as thoughts raced around his head. Memories from the past began to come together, starting with Beatrice's tearful account of several women accosting her in Amazon Mall. They had threatened to report her to the Ministry. That was when? About three months ago?

Wait a minute! Could one of her attackers in Amazon Mall have implanted something under her scalp when she'd grabbed Beatrice's head from behind?

Even if they hadn't done that, Beatrice's outburst and behaviour at the local Women's Meeting and probable failure to attend previous or subsequent monthly meetings must have resulted in her being blacklisted.

A dark shadow fell over Nick. He should have heeded Morrie's warning to stay away from Beatrice in case she was being monitored. Now, if the Island House was dismantled, he might have saved Beatrice, but in doing so, he'd be responsible for hundreds of ruined lives.

The sound of Nick's heartbeat thrashed in his ears. He showered quickly and donned a fresh shirt.

I'll do everything in my power to save the Island House, no matter what it costs.

CHAPTER TWENTY-FOUR

Nick hurried through a set of double doors, brushing past two armed, heavyset females, the orange-and-black World Federation insignia jutting from the lapels of their uniforms. They were controlling the flow of traffic into the social hall. Women, children and men took seats in neat rows in front of two lecterns. Off to one side, a woman in a jumpsuit finished setting up a tripod that held a camera with a giant display screen sticking out from the side.

Behind the lecterns, the wall was bare except for a single horizontal row of children's artwork—pastel drawings of bluebirds and yellow lions and red flowers. Sketches of happy faces and butterflies and turtles.

Nick spotted Karla, bleary-eyed, in the corner of the room. His heart leapt. She wore her usual navy blue suit. Their eyes met. Her upper lip was contorted, and her stiff posture bespoke resignation, as if her entire past connection with Nick had been wiped out. Nick took a step toward her, then stopped. Karla's eyes glowered. Nick lowered his head, some of his resolve slipping away.

He scanned the room looking for Beatrice. He didn't see her.

At precisely 6:00 p.m., Dr. Stone approached one of the lecterns with confident steps. She wore a white jacket with sizable shoulder pads over a creased gold shirt.

She cleared her throat and pointed a commanding finger at the camera crew. "Our future is near—oh, so very, very near." And then, turning and looking straight at Karla, she sneered. "Congratulations. Seems like your baby brother, barely a month into his employment with us, has led us to the kingpin's lair."

Nick's mind raced as murmurs swept across the room. He was...Karla's brother? Karla was his sister? What? How?

Karla, standing a few feet behind Dr. Stone, scowled at her boss. She shifted from one foot to another, then stepped forward. "Yes, Nick. I'm your older sister. We were separated when you were four."

"Whaaat?" Nick said, almost choking. He had taken up a position in the front row of the assembly and could hear her clearly. A few gasps came from the rows behind.

Karla related, in a detached tone of voice, how their father had deserted their mother, who had then died from a drug overdose; how Auntie Lena had taken Nick and Karla into her care until she was compelled to deliver them to the Children's Centre, where she had later secured a job. Auntie Lena had to hide the fact that she was their aunt and had donned a wig and tinted glasses and called herself Angelina so Nick wouldn't suspect. While Karla spoke, the camera crew rotated the camera from her to Nick and back.

Every fibre of Nick's being tingled with bewilderment. Something precious, something he hadn't known he had, had been concealed from him.

"She's...dying," he finally said.

Karla took three steps toward Nick, piercing him with her unflinching grey eyes. "I visited Auntie at Franklin House when you were in the hospital." Her lips thinned and her eyes narrowed. "I managed to convince her not to tell you our secret."

She took a deep breath. "Ever since I lived in the Children's Centre, I believed in the Movement, and as an adult I devoted every bit of energy to help change the world. But I always felt a shadow of doubt. A part of me—I'm ashamed to admit—still longed for family ties." She thrust out her chin. "And that's why I've kept in touch with you, Nick. I wanted to know, to *feel*, what it's like having a brother." Karla paused. "It's over. You betrayed me."

"I—I just wanted to know the truth. To help Beatrice. I wanted to..."

Karla's chin snapped down, and she locked eyes with Nick. "You spied on my boss."

Her words were acid in his face.

"I extended my hand to you, and you spat on it."

Nick stared at the floor, tracing the patterns in the hardwood, unable to speak. Had he done wrong by hacking into Dr. Stone's account?

"I've lost all trust in you. Your being my brother means zero."

Nick felt like a condemned criminal.

Karla continued. "I'm glad it happened, though, as I've learned my lesson. How you behaved toward me confirms—"

"Enough, Karla, dear," Dr. Stone interjected. "We're here to discuss the Island House, which is one *enormous* deception." She scanned the audience, then faced the camera.

"Citizens of the world! Freedom of speech, we know, is the bedrock of a moral and healthy society." She spoke clearly, taking her time with each word. "As the Advisor is fond of saying, allowing for idiotic perspectives to be aired ultimately protects against tyranny and oppression." She pushed her shoulders back. "So, rather than ordering mass arrests and shutting down this facility immediately, I have agreed, in the spirit of opennesss, to allow the executive director a chance to provide an explanation to us, and to the world via satellite, for this... this...*house of abominations.*"

Nick's head was spinning. The walls closed in. He turned and caught sight of Beatrice, who had arrived late. She was standing behind the back row, hands planted firmly on her hips, her pale face turned upward in defiance.

Mrs. Fullerfaith took her time approaching the second lectern. Her gait was steady, her face grave. She held up her hands with palms out, as if to fend off Dr. Stone's earlier accusation.

"Friends, Dr. Stone used the word *deception*. There is no greater deception than the Children's Centres. They are insidious institutions that can never replace the family. The Centres raise hollow individuals—people with poor self-esteem and stunted emotions, people who feel little connection to others. This condition renders them confused and unhappy."

Nick pressed his lips together. The Children's Centre had scarred him for life. Robbed him and his entire generation of a wholesome upbringing. Rage welled inside him—at the administrators of the centres, at the government, at the Advisor.

"The facilitators may teach honesty, discipline, prudence, manners—but there is an absence of real love," continued Mrs. Fullerfaith. "You can't pay someone to love a child. And love is the most important ingredient for producing healthy and productive members of society."

Mrs. Fullerfaith turned toward Dr. Stone and extended her arms. "I plead with you, Dr. Stone, join us. We are a peaceful community. We are opposed to any form of abuse. Come learn what we teach before you draw conclusions. Stay with us for a few days. You are most welcome."

Dr. Stone, her mouth hanging open, whipped her arms in a wide arc while rolling her eyes in mockery. "Stay here? You must be joking," she said with a laugh and then snapped to attention. She swiveled on her red stilettos toward Mrs. Fullerfaith. "This facility is not only a haven for criminals, but an Ivy League school of crime. I will not spend even an hour longer than necessary in this building." She stamped her foot. The microphones picked up the sound, and it echoed around the large auditorium. "It represents everything we oppose in our modern, civilized world."

A whistle blasted. Heads turned. It was Dmitri, a few rows behind Nick, his lips wrapped around the tips of his forefingers. Pulling his hands away from his mouth, he gave two thumbs up as an amused smile crept across his ruddy complexion.

Mrs. Fullerfaith, ignoring the interjection, looked straight into the camera. "Then arrest me and my staff but leave the residents alone. Let the media interview the children and their parents. Let the court of public opinion judge whether they are truly happy."

Dr. Stone's eyes darkened. The large, global feedback display on the side of the camera indicated a sudden surge of popular approval for Mrs. Fullerfaith.

"That's a wonderful idea. Let's test public opinion, right here and now." She motioned to two of her armed escorts. "Go bring me a child." She looked at the faces in the crowd and pointed to a girl sitting in the row behind Nick, a child of seven or eight with a button nose and braided chestnut hair. "Bring her."

Numerous cries broke out. A guard pulled the child away from her mother, and Nick heard the woman say, "Stop, you can't..." But her husband pulled her back into her seat, telling her to be patient. He reassured his wife, telling her he was only feet away from the stage and would not let anyone or anything harm their daughter. Dr. Stone smiled sweetly and motioned to the camera once more.

"Did you see that?" She pointed to the weeping mother and the father with his arms around her. "Did you see how that man pulled that woman back down and is forcing her to stay where he commands her to?"

Angry shouts erupted from the audience, and Dr. Stone held up her hands. "Now, now, please try to be civil, people. I am doing my best to give you a chance to make your case. And you're not helping yourselves with your unruly behaviour."

She motioned to the child, who had been ushered to the side of the stage, to join her. "That's right, dear. Come stand with me. I'll make sure you get a nice, sweet treat when we're done." The little girl didn't move. She stared at the odd contraption with the bags and part of a blue tube protruding from the back of Dr. Stone's jacket. "Oh, are you afraid of me because of this old thing?"

Dr. Stone turned toward the camera again.

"As everyone knows, it's not just women and children that have been victimized in family-based societies, but our entire species." She studied the audience through narrowed eyes. "I ask you! How much science, philosophy and art was never developed? How many female geniuses never realized their potential? Humanity could have conquered the galaxy by now."

She stepped closer to the camera, gasping to regain her composure. "This device I am forced to wear on my back, day and night—and which has frightened this darling young girl—" She put her clenched fist to her chest and emitted a rasping cough. "It filters the air in my lungs. I am certain doctors would have been able to cure me if, for most of our history, medical research was not the monopoly of only half the population.

"Fellow humans! Today, as the Hardinians are stoking the flames of rebellion, the family is again on trial. The question before us is simple. Does the institution of the family bring out the best in people or the worst? Do we go back to the way things were—to patriarchy, oppression, raising generation after generation of damaged souls?"

Dr. Stone paused. She appeared to be having difficulty breathing. She motioned again to the little girl to come. However, the child remained firmly rooted in place at the edge of the platform, with her fist against her mouth, a guard blocking her return to her parents. The girl was scanning the audience, forlorn, her eyes puffy and red.

Unexpectedly, Dr. Stone turned away from the child, extended her arms to the audience and spoke calmly.

"On one point we can agree—people seem to have an instinctive feeling of connection and responsibility toward relatives. The Hardinians say this is proof that the family is a natural and healthy thing."

Nick tilted his head, attentive to Dr. Stone's every word and facial expression.

She continued. "Now reflect: What I'm going to say doesn't apply to those of us who grew up in the Children's Centres, free from moms and dads, brothers and sisters, aunts and uncles. But for the older ones, Why is it we might feel responsibility toward our younger siblings or our children?" She paused, as if allowing her imaginary lecture hall students to brace themselves for the answer.

"It's because they grew up with us. We witnessed their most private moments—when they wet their beds, when they were caught in a lie. We were exposed to their secrets, their fears, their desires. This intimate knowledge was entirely circumstantial, of course, yet it created a sense of connection and responsibility, however false.

"As for older siblings and parents, we need them for our therapy." She bent toward the camera. "As everyone knows, they are almost always the cause of our insecurities, our phobias, our anxieties. We *need* the people who damaged us so we can repair the relationships, so we can help them correct their wrongs."

She straightened and stabbed the air with her index finger. "The girl who was abused by her father longs for him to recognize the damage he has done and will go to the ends of the earth to ensure it happens." With that, she turned and looked at the little girl, the camera following her gaze. The screen was filled with the young child's tear-stained cheeks.

Nick punched a fist against his thigh. What an evil thing to say! She had implied this young girl's fear came from being abused by her father. Anger boiled inside Nick's chest. Evidently he wasn't alone. Many in the audience were standing, and two armed guards restrained the child's father, preventing him from getting out of his seat.

But Dr. Stone continued with her lecture as though nothing untoward was occurring.

Nick looked at Karla; her face was ashen.

"Furthermore, our children tend to look like us. It gives us a smug sense of immortality."

Hmm. How astute, thought Nick. *If it wasn't for her distorted perspective, Dr. Stone could be teaching in the School of Life.*

"There are other reasons why the family was once considered important. Funerals? Weddings? Holidays?" Her voice rose to a singsong at the end of each word. "Knowing we'd face the same individuals over a span of many years, we'd make a special effort to be on good terms with them. There was also the prospect of inheritance..." As she spoke, her eyes shifted again to the feedback display, and for a fleeting moment, she smiled.

"There's more!" she bellowed, clenching her fists. "People were legally obligated to raise their children.

"Imagine: twenty years ripped out of the prime of your life! But what if your child was born deaf or blind or with a respiratory condition like I have? What if the baby had Down syndrome, or spina bifida? Or how about esophageal atresia? Microcephaly? Omphalocele? There's no shortage of serious birth defects that would cause a parent's life to be *completely* ruined. Today, thanks to the Children's Centres, we're free of these burdens and these fears.

"Also, parents were historically a repository of knowledge, advice and guidance. Today we have Netbots."

Nick turned his head. He was amazed at how quickly the dozens of women, children and men who filled the social hall had fallen quiet. Some of the children were pressed against their mothers' bosoms, others were sprawled on the floor, still others stood with hands on hips, squinting at Dr. Stone. Everyone seemed to be trying to make sense of what they were hearing.

"To the Hardinian sympathizers, I plead with you, reflect on the kind of world you want. It's not just—"

"I'm sorry, Dr. Stone," interjected Mrs. Fullerfaith, "but I must make it clear we are not Hardinians and disavow any affiliation—"

"Semantics!" Dr. Stone spun toward Mrs. Fullerfaith, thrusting an index finger at her. "Either you draw your inspiration from the past, or you draw it from the future." The gold-coloured bracelet around her wrist jingled and shimmered as she spoke. She turned back to the audience.

Then she froze. Unexpectedly, her face relaxed. She clasped her hands together in front of her body and spoke with great calmness. "With the powers invested in me as an Enforcer for the World Federation, I hereby order all staff and all residents in this building be arrested immediately."

Nick's chest tightened with intense anger. Feelings, thoughts and images bombarded his consciousness. Miss Laura in the Children's Centre saying to him, "You feel day after day like an empty shell—like you're nobody and belong nowhere." Lying in the hospital bed, planning his suicide. Beatrice crying on the bench in Amazon Mall. Angelina's icy grip on his hand as she announced she didn't want to die among strangers. Morrie dancing with his children in a circle. The classes at the Island House, how illuminating they were and how happy he'd felt here.

He stood up and yelled, "You're a liar! You said you'd let these people make their case. Leave us in peace." At that point, men and women began running up to the stage shouting, "Liar! liar!" and "Leave us in peace!" a few shaking a fist at Dr. Stone.

In the blink of an eye, Nick saw Karla standing next to Dr. Stone, saying something to her while gesticulating intently.

Mayhem engulfed the auditorium. Dr. Stone thrust an arm out to keep Karla at a distance and yelled into the microphone, "Everyone against the side walls, now!" Within seconds, a dozen female law enforcement officials, guns in hand, arranged themselves in a straight line across the centre of the auditorium. One of them fired two warning shots into the air. Men and women yelped. Children cried. A muscular, dark-skinned man scurried toward the exit, two diapered infants pressed against his chest, side by side.

"Don't ruin their futures," he bellowed, as he approached the two female officers guarding the doors. "Please, let us through!"

One of the officers pointed a gun at his abdomen and ordered him to stop, but the man continued his advance. A shot rang out, and the man staggered backward, grunted and collapsed onto the floor, still clutching the infants. Several women who stood close by rushed over and knelt beside him, one of them reaching for the crying babies.

Beatrice dashed in the wounded man's direction but was blocked by the small crowd that had formed around him. She turned and caught Nick's eye.

"This is all my fault," Nick cried, approaching her with trembling legs.

"No, Nick. You tried to do the right thing," Beatrice said, panting. "You showed courage. You saved my life and have given me hope."

Nick stepped closer to Beatrice. He peered into her eyes. They were beautiful. He had never noticed, but they were azure, like a summer sky.

Nego Huzcotoq

"I love you," Beatrice said, her face wet with tears.

Two officers grabbed their arms from behind. As they separated Beatrice from Nick, he wrenched one arm free, reached out and stroked her cheek. "I never knew what love meant, Beatrice. But I do now. I love you too."

CHAPTER TWENTY-FIVE

"You have a visitor!" the guard bellowed, her ruddy face pressed against the bars of the tiny window in the door.

Nick's neck muscles tensed. He was in no mood for more visits from loquacious social workers trying to persuade him to abandon his "perverted" views about family.

He balled his fists and felt his biceps respond. His workouts, even in this cramped space, were beginning to achieve results. One day—he didn't know how—he would escape from his wrongful confinement.

As mandated by the Ottawa Jail policy, he took a seat on the rough wooden bench and faced the cell door, waiting.

Karla entered and stood in front of him, eyes downcast. She sported a baggy brown sweater over a long blue-jean skirt. Her hair hung unkempt over her shoulders. Her face was pale with a few patches of rough skin around her cheekbones.

Nick sat quietly, a grim twist to his mouth.

"How're they treating you?" Karla asked.

A splinter from the bench pricked the back of Nick's thigh, and he shifted his leg. He lowered his head into his hands, partially concealing his unshaven face as he dug his elbows into his still fleshy thighs. He felt the tingle of Karla's stare on the backs of his hands and wished she would leave.

"I visited Auntie Lena at Franklin House yesterday."

Nick didn't respond.

"She died last night—apparently soon after I left. Her final words to me were...about you."

Nick squeezed his eyes closed. *Angelina. Oh, no!*

"She said, 'Please take good care of Nico. If you can, tell him his mother and father and I loved him dearly.'"

The last time Nick had seen Angelina had been in her apartment, when she'd disclosed her grim prognosis. Instead of crying, he'd been somewhat relieved! Yes, a cold, heartless relief that he wouldn't have to visit her too many more times.

And yet, her dying thought had been about his welfare.

Nick pressed a palm against his runny nose. Why had Karla revealed that his aunt and his parents had loved him? From Karla's perspective, what difference should that make?

Cold defiance crept through Nick—a desire to challenge this woman whose intellect he'd been in awe of ever since he could remember.

He sat up, displaying his face and scruffy beard. "What difference does that make?"

Karla stared at her hands.

Nick heaved himself to his feet and looked down at her bowed head. Funny, he had never appreciated, in all these years, that he was a head taller than her. With a jerk of his chin, he motioned toward the cot near the metal door, inviting her to sit. Karla wavered, then plopped down in the middle of the cement floor, causing a faint plume of dust to rise into the air.

Nick resumed his seat on the wooden bench and crossed his arms.

Karla remained silent and didn't make eye contact. Nick narrowed his eyes to slits. "So, now that I know we're related, am I suddenly supposed to feel differently toward you? Do I owe you something for leaving our mother's womb in good working order for me?"

Karla's gaze wandered across the floor. "I can't tell you what you're supposed to feel, Nick. And, no, you don't owe me anything. Not even friendship."

Nick slammed his hands down on the bench. Through clenched teeth, he said, "Then please leave."

Karla sat still for a long moment, then struggled to her feet. She shifted from one foot to the other.

"Nick, I—Doreeta was wrong. She shouldn't have shut down the Island House. I just want you to know—"

Nick leaned back against the damp cell wall. In rising tones, he said, "Then why didn't you stop her?"

"What?"

"You could've said something."

"I was confused."

"Confused? About what?"

"Everything. What I believed in. What I stood for."

Nick looked away. When he spoke again, his voice was low and measured. "Why did you visit Angelina?"

Karla released a slow sigh and lowered herself back onto the floor. "Nick, Auntie Lena and I have always kept in touch. I tried to deny the relationship, telling myself we were just friends who happened to be related. Deep down, I knew I was deceiving myself." She looked up at Nick. "I've been deceiving myself my entire life. I...I always yearned for the love and closeness of a family." Tears welled in Karla's eyes.

Nick sat up straight. He'd never seen Karla cry. Her tears reminded him of his encounter with Beatrice in the mall. She, too, had cried after opening up to him. He reached to the side of his pants for a tissue and then remembered jail garb didn't have pockets.

Karla was sobbing now, prompting an unexpected feeling of tenderness in Nick's heart. The miserable woman in a heap on the floor was a member of his family. His sister.

He cleared his throat. "Why didn't you and Aunt Lena want me to know we were related?"

Karla slowly lifted her head and looked at Nick through her tears. "When Auntie was forced to deliver you to the Children's Centre, you weren't even five, an age when family can be forgotten without much consequence. And when you grew up, we felt it would be wrong"—her voice cracked—"to burden you with your past."

Nick's stomach clenched. *Burden me with my past?* He drew in a slow, even breath. "We've become a society of orphans. Cut off from our parents, our grandparents, culture, traditions, beliefs…"

Karla slid along the floor to Nick and grasped his hand. She glanced at the eclipse symbol tattooed on the back of his hand and pressed it against her wet cheek, her tears spilling over the black and orange circles. Between sniffles, she said, "The government thinks heaven has no roots, but it does."

Karla's words washed over Nick, and in a flash, the realization hit him. This was the ultimate goal of the Movement: to create a heaven on earth by first severing humanity from its roots.

It was not a movement the government had created. It was not a movement led by a dictator or despot. It was not even a movement that had been started solely by women. It was, rather, a movement of an entire species frustrated with the intractable problem of men—what to do with them, how to tame them, how to prevent them from destroying the world.

And it was a movement that, like all utopian movements throughout history, believed it would succeed.

Our strength depends on our roots, Morrie had said.

Nick recalled the big red oak behind Morrie's house. The tree reached into the ground and up toward the sky, and Nick imagined the roots going even deeper and the red oak branching out even farther and reaching ever higher and higher, all the way to heaven.

Nick pulled his hand from Karla's grasp. "I'm sorry I spied on Dr. Stone."

Karla turned and looked into his eyes. "Doreeta and I are no longer together."

"Even so, it was wrong—"

"Nick, you've been fighting a war, a war against dehumanization of men. Sometimes warriors have to break rules."

Nick shook his head. "I've always considered truthfulness the most important virtue, and like a fool, I violated my own principle."

"Nick, you violated your own principle *for the sake* of truth. You were—are—a maverick."

Nick reached out to Karla's face and gave it a gentle pat. She smiled and Nick stood, pulling Karla up with him. He felt strong. "Okay, where do we go from here?"

Karla paused. "I don't know. Maybe the Progressives are onto something. What was your experience at the Island House?"

"It was an oasis. The Progressives believe it's possible to raise healthy families without falling into a cycle of violence and abuse. It's a matter of reaching back into age-old teachings."

"But historically—"

"Still, their goals and methods are our best hope. At least, as a starting point."

Karla glanced around and cringed. "Nick, you've been in this smelly cage almost three weeks. All the residents of the Island House, including the administrators, have been dispersed across the US and Canada and are in custody awaiting trial in their various jurisdictions. It'll take years for those trials to get underway, and in the meantime the governments are happy to let you all rot in jail."

Nick squirmed. "Can you use your connections—"

"I resigned from the Ministry two days ago."

Nick turned his head to the side. He paced around the eight-by-ten-foot cell. "We need to find

Mrs. Fullerfaith. She's probably in jail somewhere. We'll need her advice."

"How are you going to get out? You're a magician, not an escape art—"

"*You'll* have to find her then. And quickly. The world needs to rethink everything—parenting, Children's Centres, the Rite of Passage..."

Karla took a deep breath. "There's something else."

"What is it?"

"The Hardinians—they've—the insurrection has started."

"What?" Nick's heart raced.

"They seized control of an air base in South Carolina this morning. The US president has declared a nationwide state of emergency."

"Anything here in Canada? Other countries?"

"Not yet, but the Advisor has put the World Federation on the highest alert."

Nick swallowed. If the insurrection led to civil war, which side would he be on? The Hardinians would take humanity back to the Age of Oppression. Hadn't Morrie said the Hardinians had a distorted perspective about family, about parental rights and responsibilities? And hadn't Mrs. Fullerfaith said something similar? On the other hand, the government's ideology was just as twisted. He leaned against the damp wall. What would

Morrie do? Was he still in a coma? Mrs. Fullerfaith had said the Hardinians claimed responsibility for his brutal assault.

Would Morrie and Mrs. Fullerfaith support the government? Likely. At least there was democracy. Rule of law. Freedom of speech. The Hardinians would establish a dictatorship.

Karla touched Nick's shoulder, and he turned to her. "I'm sorry, Nick. My fifteen minutes are almost up. And they told me they won't grant me another visit with you. They found out we're siblings."

Karla reached into her purse. She pulled out a small white envelope and handed it to Nick. Nick opened it and gazed at a photo of a little girl and a little boy sitting one behind the other on a rocking horse in a playground.

"It's us, before we were separated." Karla said. "You were three and a half; I was about six."

Nick peered into the eyes of the little boy: soft and brown, radiating wonder. He shifted his gaze to the little girl's face, her thin lips squeezed together in an expression of determination.

Nick wanted to go back in time and visit those children. Talk to them, ask them questions.

He held the photo out to Karla, raising his eyebrows.

"I want you to have it," she said.

Nick tightened his hold on the photo. "They—we—look so happy."

Karla leaned in. "Who knows?" she said, her eyes sparkling. "Maybe one day, you'll have children of your own and I'll have children of my own and they'll play together in the park just like you and I once did. And they'll grow up happy."

Children of my own? Nick's heart hammered in his chest, as it had done every time he'd thought of Beatrice since they'd been forcibly separated: how she looked up to him, trusted him and had now endeared herself to him. She must be in another jail cell, maybe also in Ottawa. He hoped she wasn't too far away.

Nick looked Karla in the eyes. "Can you…I mean, would you do some research and find out where Beatrice is being held and see if you can visit her? And then tell her I plan to come get her and that…that…"

"That you want to marry her?" Her voice bubbled over.

Nick's neck and face turned hot. "Yes." He swallowed. "The sooner the better."

He leaned toward his sister and embraced her.

Ingram Content Group UK Ltd.
Milton Keynes UK
UKHW011810040723
424531UK00004B/213

9 781738 678105